I0620230

MARIAH'S PROLOGUES

GRACE BRIDGES

STORIES FROM THE WORLD OF BELFAST 2079

Mariah's Prologues
ISBN: 978-1927154496

With editorial support from:
Liberty Speidel • Barbara Hartzler • J. L. L. Davis • Dan T. Davis
T. J. Akers • Bokerah Brumley • Bethany Jennings • Jodhan Ford
Ashley Joy • Teddi Deppner • Sharon Rose Miller

Published by
Splashdown Books,
New Zealand
www.splashdownbooks.com

www.gracebridges.kiwi

contents

the Dog With no name

Perhaps the dog had had a name, once, long ago, when children christened the puppy they'd begged for. Perhaps it had been Christmas, with shiny baubles hung on a fragrant tree, or somebody's birthday, and he had burst out of a barely-wrapped box with the same brown ears and grey patches that he still wore, to be greeted with delight by the little ones and a certain disapproval on the part of a busybody aunt.

He almost remembered his name, through the haze of babyhood when he had been the centre of their attention, but now he had not heard the name in so long that he would not know it if he heard it. No doubt in the beginning they had called him by it a hundred times a day, called him to play or snuggle or eat. Nobody had spoken that name now for years.

The good times were long gone, those days before they'd grown tired of cherishing him, had sunk into the virtual worlds of their gaming consoles and the concerns that their attire be exactly as calculated and slovenly as that of their peers.

They didn't care for the dog now grown to full size and having lost his infant cuteness, the inherent puppyness that had made them ooh and aah and tickle his little grey-speckled belly, the playfulness now tempered into a fondness for fetching sticks—of whose throwing they quickly wearied.

Their mother was gone, their father too often drank his pay and yet it was he who fed and walked the family pet. Between the two was a familiarity that fell some distance short of friendship. He called the dog by many names: mangy cur, fleabag, bloody mutt, or son of a bitch, if he felt like being funny—but there was no real name among the varied appellations. So the dog went on well enough without.

As they wandered the streets of Belfast late at night, the man with a bottle in one hand and in the other the frayed old rope that served as a leash, it was the dog who knew the way home although his master did not like to let him lead. Something to do with being the one in charge for once, although he had lost control of everything he had ever called his own, so now he domineered over the dog who was not really his but his children's, whom he could no longer control.

The man had a real name of course, but it was never heard on these nightly excursions as the booze loosened his tongue and he groaned to himself at the ruin of his life. The mournful sound echoed down back alleys and along brick-fronted terraces wherever he went.

Residents in the houses he passed would awaken, shuffle to their windows and open them with varying creaks according to difficulty and age of the structure—maintenance was not a priority in this part of town, or indeed any part nowadays—and they would stand there in their faded nightshirts and shout at him. "Move along there, ya wastrel! Bleedin' idjit." They called him many more names besides.

He was particularly enraged this night because his teenage son had defied him, or so he thought—the boy refused to go fetch a few beers from the store—but he muttered as he went, about kids these days and the sheer nerve of it all. Surely it had not been an unreasonable request of his. After all, he had always required the youngsters to go and buy what he needed, never mind what it was. And now to be rebuffed all of a sudden?

The nerve of it, indeed. He was so angry that he had forgotten to feed the dog his customary scraps, little enough as that would have been. The dog had missed meals before and did not mind so much; perhaps he would beg something from the man-child on returning home. There were worse things, to be sure.

It was close to curfew and they would have to be safe home or risk being targeted by Senate guards, perhaps even one of those notoriously brutal cyborgs that were supposed to have arrived in town some years ago to lend their support in subduing the discontented rabble; it was said an infringer discovered by a cyborg was unlikely to survive the encounter. Still, if they were really here, they were rarely seen.

His master stumbled down a mews, drained the last drop from his bottle, cursed and flung it to the ground. For a fraction of a moment it spun and glinted in the night air, then it shattered in the culvert, sending shards in every direction.

The smash of glass echoed back and forth between the decrepit walls. A window opened with a thud that indicated it needed a fair amount of encouragement to do so; an old one's voice rang out in sharp displeasure. "Ya drunk hobo! Gerroutofit."

The man staggered out into the street, tugging the hungry dog behind him. A few steps was all he could manage before he had to stop and get his balance. When he had done so, he bestowed upon the leash a particularly hard yank, just because, so that there was a yelp. "Shurrup, ya mongrel," he slurred, and backhanded the cowering animal in the neck. The dog retreated as far as the rope would allow. He stared sadly at his master's feet. He had no choice, no other upon whom to confer his loyalty.

"Hey," came a new voice, "Ease up on the poor fella, why don't ya?"

A woman—prowling the streets at night—what new thing was this? The dog had never seen the like before. He eyed her carefully. Friend or foe? Now she walked towards them with silent steps, her face still shadowed. The dog growled half-heartedly, for show, because he knew he should, but he did not really mean it.

The drunk considered her presence pure insanity. He attempted to roll up his sleeves and prepared to give her what for, as soon as he could locate her in his blurred vision. He turned, tripped on a cracked kerb, barely righted himself, then caught sight of figures in the pooled glow under the weak streetlight. Oh. She wasn't alone, then, this bold one. He squinted at her older companion and back at her: so alike in the face, they had to be related. The father, if that was who he was, stepped forward, and with him the shadow of another dog.

Before he could be stopped, the dog with no name strained forward to touch noses with the other, a collie who stood at taut attention, tail high. Her long hair had been conscientiously groomed and hung shiny from her flanks.

Motionless, the collie saw before her a mostly-brown dog of medium build, with hand-sized brindled grey and whitish patches scattered here and there across his coat. She sniffed his unwashed scent with disdain. He probably had fleas. Yet she rarely met another dog in this world become strange; even this lanky pauper was a brother of sorts to her.

"Good girl, Jemima," said the father, a cautioning hand laid on her combed withers.

His daughter moved nearer so that the whites of her eyes became visible. "Shame on ye for hitting a noble beast like that. You don't deserve him."

The voice was kind, awaking doggy dreams of better days and compassionate friends now all but forgotten. The nameless one thought he'd rather like to go home with someone like this. Perhaps she might feed him warm food and doze with him in front of a cosy fire. His empty innards rumbled then, so loud he was sure the whole world must hear it.

The woman spoke again, even more gently. "Look at those big brown eyes. He'd stay with you till the end of the world, if you treat him right." Wishing she could take him home and coddle him, that she could simply relieve this villain of the leash and walk away with a new companion, she crouched and extended a hand.

The dog didn't dare approach for fear of his master. He simply looked into her eyes for a moment that seemed to go on forever. Again he imagined that fantastical future with humans as dedicated to him as he was to them, humans with whom he could be together. It was all he had ever wanted—well, aside from a full stomach.

The trance was broken by the drunk vomiting down his shirt. A cloud of stink wafted about the street while he spat the dregs at his feet. No sooner had he cleared his mouth again but he set forth to lambast the world in general and the persons before him in particular. "This—this country's gone to rot. And ye—ye're disturbing the peace and harassing innocent citizens!" He raised a trembling finger. "I'll warrant it'd be your type who'd commit treason to overthrow the government, so ye would." Privately, he himself thought he wouldn't mind in the slightest if that happened, since it was the government's fault it had come to this state of affairs.

At length, having used up all the invective his brain could currently hold, he wobbled in a half-circle, gripped the leash, and departed the scene.

From the corner, the dog looked back and glimpsed the woman with her father and the blessed, lucky Jemima, standing there watching them go. It was a light in his darkness that such considerate people— such well-loved dogs—even existed, and here on the dank streets of night-time Belfast, no less. A painful yank on the neck set the dog facing forward again; he sighed, and trotted after his pitiable human.

They skulked through the restless, sleeping city, the dog taking the lead at each intersection to ensure they kept heading for home. He did so unobtrusively, so as to avoid being punished for knowing more than his master, however simple that task given the man's current state. Just a slight lean to go this way, and a large curve to take that corner, step by precarious step—in this way they crossed the neighbourhoods and rounded a number of Peace Walls that blocked off streets between sworn enemies who had likely never met, the feud inherited from their fathers.

The man paused, squatted, scrabbled in the gutter and drew out an unbroken bottle, which he held up to the light. Finding it empty, he let forth a barrage of epithets and let it fall again. Once more the crash of breaking glass resounded in the street, once more windows groaned and more nightshirted inhabitants shouted their displeasure at him from bedroom heights. "Begone, ye woeful excuse for a human!"

Now the dog had seen his master in many a bad state, but never so bad as this, for all the money was gone and so was all the drink he'd hoarded for a rainy day. The withdrawal was hitting him hard. His eye fell upon his faithful dog, and he snarled. "What are you looking at, ye great moron?" The dog only continued to watch him with concern. The man grew more enraged and set about spanking the dog's flanks with the flat of his palm. At first the dog flinched, but the blows were careless and badly aimed; he danced about, avoiding them where he could and hoping for an end. But the man raged on and the hands became fists. Finally, blinded by madness, he lost his grip on the rope leash in order to pummel with both hands.

The dog hesitated for a moment, remembering the whole of his young life with that family, but as fists rose again to strike him, self-preservation finally kicked in. He turned and fled away, not looking back, ignoring the angry shouts that now followed him, knowing that the man would never be able to catch him in his condition. The timbre of the cries changed from a holler to a whimper as he ran; perhaps it was just the increasing distance. "That's my dog—My—Come back here, ya great git—Dog!" Then the voice was gone.

He sped the length of several streets, not caring what direction he took. Away was all that mattered. His thoughts massed, confused, one moment wishing he could go back, the next rejecting that idea as foolhardy and dangerous in view of the punishment that would certainly await him if he found his way home.

The rope fluttered from his neck like a flag but he barely noticed it. Nobody saw his headlong flight except for a grandfather hunched at his curtainless first-floor window. The old man silently wished happiness on the distressed beast, for he'd had a dog once, too. A work-hardened hand flicked away an unwelcome tear as the observer turned his back on the view.

The dog with no name dashed mindlessly past row after row of houses joined wall to wall, each set almost exactly like the last with its crumbling stonework, flaking paint, and cracked windowpanes under a hodge-podge of hastily patched tile roofs with chimneys that variously stood straight or askew.

Each sheltered a sleeping family or two, usually several more bodies than had been planned in such a home, for times were hard and things weren't as they used to be. Even so, shelter was easier to come by than food.

Every door hid hunger, every garden patch was dead or dying thanks to genetic experiments run amuck. The terminator gene: invented for profit, now slowly proving fatal to every living thing—with the possible exception of weeds and the simplest sort of grasses. But the dog couldn't eat those.

Topmost in his mind was the desire to find the woman who had been kind to him earlier in the evening. He well remembered her scent, and searched for it in every street he passed through. There was no doubt that she would feed him and caress him and let him sleep by the fire. Then there was her dog...Oh, Jemima. His heart beat a little faster at the thought of that fine dame. Would she even deign to look at him again, she of the shiny clean coat and privileged position? He pined as he searched. Surely she would come to like him, if he could only find her again.

Finally he slowed and felt a pressing need to get out of plain sight, away from the open street where anyone might see him, catch him, abuse him. He spied a narrow gap between a leafless hedge and a wall, and pushed his way through—bits of brick crumbled away and scraped over his fur on one side. Then he found himself in the house yard beyond.

He came face to face with a boy of about eight who sat there on the back step of the home, the late hour notwithstanding. Angry voices burst from the kitchen window.

"Why did you have to take that job in the first place?"

"They promised more food. Listen, they're not asking that much more of me…"

"Not that much more! That bossy one wants to get the shift on you, mark my words."

"Willnae happen again, I swear. She just sorta…snuck up on me."

"Stop the noise and shut yer hole."

So it went on. The dog and the boy shared a look of mutual understanding.

The dog approached, sensing no malice in the child, who began sliding his hands over the dog's face and neck. The cuffs of the child's felted woollen jacket, vaguely cardigan-shaped, swept the tips of the dog's hair; a garment sewn from an old blanket, for the shortage of food also brought with it poverty in other areas.

The probing fingers found the rope and set about worrying at the knot. Hardened by age, it resisted at first. The dog couldn't remember a time when it hadn't been upon his neck. After a long while, and with admirable persistence on the part of the boy, it loosened and the mess of strands fell to the bare ground. The dog regarded it curiously—the last vestige of the life he knew.

The boy fondled his ears as the shouting died away inside the house. He would like to have a dog of his own, a friend to play with—for the local kids were all a little older than him and spent long days in the factories, returning at night too exhausted to kick a ball around the street as they used to do. He looked into the dog's face and found acceptance there. If he couldn't have human friends any more, perhaps the dog would stay around.

The back door was yanked open and the mother seized her son by the collar she'd stitched herself out of that blanket. Her grip loosened just a smidge at the thought that she might tear his clothing, for it was the only jacket he had. How hopeful she'd been on the day she'd sewn it, hopeful that she and her husband could provide for the family, hopeful even that someday, the shortages would pass.

And now? There was less food than ever, given reluctantly by harried bosses, not near enough to live on. Not even when her man had been playing around with that one. Bitter pain hardened to iron within her. She dragged the child inside, his arms flailing, without her even noticing the dog.

The door slammed; silence reigned once more. The night pricked with stars and dew, a thing of wonder. The dog's breath steamed the air and he curled up against the side of the house. He didn't know where else to go and he'd like to see the boy again; it was clear the child was kind, though not a word had been spoken between them. For a few short minutes he allowed himself to imagine again the scenario in front of that blazing fire, only this time it was the young boy he dozed with instead of the woman from the street.

But it was not to be. The husband stepped outside for a smoke and realised a stray was taking shelter in his yard. Stopping to grasp the nearest weapon, he seized upon the fallen leash-rope and snapped it about like a whip. The dog jumped to his feet and left in the same way he'd come in, scraping his other side in his precipitous exit.

He wandered the dark and quiet streets for a long time that night, learning that the world was a much bigger place than he had ever known, much harder, and much dirtier and colder as well. The dew became a dense fog and then settled into one of those solid Belfast drizzles that soaked him to the skin. He shivered, but kept moving in his search for a sheltered place to rest. There was no sound of traffic, for private vehicles had been outlawed, but a bike zipped by here and there and a few desperate souls tried to cross the city on foot even though curfew was a far distant memory by now.

As dawn's first light touched the sky above the dying forests of the

Antrim hills that girded the city on the northwest side, the dog found an open gate which led to a yard containing a burned-out house. It smelled of cinders, but it might provide a roof at least. The dog wandered through the ash and grime-filled rooms, finding no dry spot. He paused at the gap once filled by a back door and looked out.

He did not give much heed to the two-storey concrete and barbed-wire Peace Wall that loomed above the back garden. He had eyes only for the lean-to shed at its base, somehow unscathed by the house fire. Trotting through the ash and rubble, he made his way over to the shed's dark opening. Small, glittering eyes looked back at him from the blackness—but it was only rats.

Rats! A windfall for him and a chance to sate his aching hunger. Weary though he was, he summoned the energy to chase down the rodent inhabitants, and when he had made a meal of them, he settled down in his new home with a sense of hope.

Hope that he would continue to feed himself in a world that had become huge and confusing; hope for a future without abuse; and hope that one day he would find that family again, those kind humans and a beautiful mate with whom to share his days.

Then he would not be nameless any more.

MOTHERS OF BELFAST

Aileen Kelly shoved at the kitchen window in vain. Water had gotten even farther into the cracked wood during the last storm, and now it might never open again, it was that swollen. Just one more malfunction to add to the list. She sighed and turned back to the rueful mess in the sink. Water ran from the tap in a trickle, the most it ever gave, so she slowly scrubbed and scraped at the week's dishes as the paltry flow allowed. They owned a lot of dishes, which allowed for the once-weekly wash; their own crockery, and Gran's, and a good many stray pieces as well, even if most of the collection was chipped and faded.

Today had been her day off, she supposed that meant it was Sunday. Nearly over, too late to seek out a mass even if she'd had the intention, hadn't in years, who knew if there were even any still running. The household had its own representative of the church just upstairs anyway, if she was to be believed. Sitting up there praying for all their souls. Aileen snorted. The strange little nun was pretty harmless, if nun she be, and she was a nice enough person when it came down to it.

The Kelly family had moved into this house six years ago, with high hopes for the future. Brian had been two, Morna was born shortly after. Alice had followed four years later. Even Brian remembered no other home. More to the point, he remembered no better times, for these hard years had dragged on almost ever since.

Aileen would not be eating today—unless her roving husband found illicit weeds— because she was not at work. In the early days of the currency wipeout, her "wage" had consisted of enough oats and potatoes to feed the family for three or four days in a week, and Ciaran's portion had covered the remainder of the time. Sometimes there had even been a leek or a couple of onions in the packet. Now they only handed her a small scoop of oats each day, perhaps enough for one good meal for herself. Small as the portion was, she divided it into three and ate it in the evening with her two older children who grew so tall and scrawny before her eyes. Her husband's ration he shared with her mother, who did not eat very much, citing old age as the reason for a lesser appetite. No one believed her for a second.

The children's grandmother had moved in when her husband had died, some three years ago. The man had not been Aileen's father, but he treated them all well enough and Aileen had some good memories of feasts that he had provided, even sometimes with meat. Gran had simply wanted to be with family, and Ciaran had been won over by promises that she could take care of the children while both parents worked. Soon the youngsters would be old enough to go to the factories. Two were old enough now, truth be told, but Aileen wanted them to stay under the radar as long as they could. Let the Senate keep its filthy hands off her little ones.

Of course Ciaran grumbled about sharing his meagre, hard-earned lunch, but he was partly mollified that his wife managed to feed all the children—two with her ration, Alice with her milk. The milk was going to stop soon, she could feel it, could see it in her own sinking cheeks and stick-like limbs that her health would soon no longer support the nursing of a child. What they would do then, she had no idea. Already Alice had been asking for the solid food the others ate, but there was nothing left to give her.

Ciaran's brother and his sixteen-year old son also lived with them since the day last year they'd shown up on the doorstep from Dublin. Things were bad down South, he'd said, and when asked what happened to his wife, he had become unable to speak and his son had abruptly left the room. Now the two of them had found jobs to feed themselves and lived in the small front bedroom that had the crack in the wall, it having been vacated by Brian who had to share with his sisters at the back. He complained, but not about sharing a room—he said he missed the crack, said it was a magic door to another world where there was plenty of food, and he went there every night when it had been his. Gran slept on the settee although its springs were failing—she did not wish to climb the stairs, even if there had been room for her.

The last inhabitant was the nun—or at least, that's what she claimed to be. She'd come knocking all along the street three months ago, begging for a place to lay her head. The neighbours had turned her away and Aileen had been about to do the same, yet her conscience rankled. It was not right to rebuff a nun. Perhaps she wasn't a good Catholic any more, but if she took in this Reverend Mother, surely it would count in her favour. But where to put her? "I'm afraid there's only the attic," she'd said, "but you're welcome to it."

The woman's face had shone her gratitude. "God bless you, daughter," the first of many times she would apply the phrase, to the point where the children good-naturedly mimicked her behind her back. Ciaran, weighed down with the burden of feeding his family, was beyond caring about another body in the house and had simply shrugged when asked if she could stay. She, too, had a job to go to—a divine calling exempted nobody these days—but upon returning each evening she went straight up to her garret and remained there with the mice and the cobwebs; the family theorised that surely she must be doing a lot of praying.

Aileen's reminiscences were interrupted by the sound of the front door opening and closing. Ciaran had gone scouting the hidden corners of Belfast to search for edible weeds, the only things that would still grow in the thick, dead mud. Dandelions still sprouted more easily than most plants, but were quite horrible to eat, even when cooked—the larger leaves could not be completely chewed, had to be swallowed as lumps of cud-like goop, but they did put an end to hunger pains for a while.

"That you, dearest?" she called, setting down a scummy dish and turning to meet him. "Get anything?"

"A little." He showed her his pouch with some wilting leaves. It would not even feed one of them. "But look at this." He pulled out an entire dandelion plant complete with roots and one solitary bud. "We can grow it right here behind the house, and it can spread, and we can have our own supply."

Aileen plastered on a smile, but her heart sank because for today, there was nothing. Bitter and tough as they were, dandelion leaves were filling, and right then she could have demolished that plant he held—all by herself. Her stomach rumbled and she laid a hand across it without realising she did so.

Ciaran set the plant down on the table. "I know you're hungry, love. Listen, Alan told me a place we might find more food, but I need your help..."

Aileen lost concentration as Ciaran spoke. Her stomach hurt, her breasts hurt too, she would have to feed Alice soon but how could she when everything was so empty? Her head swam.

"...and if the guards don't spy us, we'll get a grand haul!" Ciaran finished.

Wait. Guards? "Sorry, can you run that past me again?"

Ciaran grimaced. "Apparently a boatload of food gets tossed in back of police HQ every day. They're trying to make compost, rejuvenate the soil with scraps, but they won't miss a few bucketloads, right?"

"Aren't there cyborgs there? Enhanced senses?" Aileen had never seen one of the augmented humans, but by all accounts they were fast and brutal.

"Not many. Most are stationed farther south, I think." Dublin, of course, where his brother's wife had met her end, perhaps at the metal hand of one of those monsters.

"All—all right. I'll go with you." Danger was justified if it meant the family could eat.

"Go where?" It was the nun, carrying her chamber-pot to empty in the downstairs bathroom.

Ciaran chuckled without humour. "Hello, Mother Tangerine." She said her name was Clementine, but he claimed he never could tell the difference, least of all now, when no one had seen either fruit for years. "Come if you want—the more the merrier. We're going to relieve the Senate's forces of some edibles."

The mother's eyes gleamed. "I'm in! Be with you in a jiffy." She shuffled over to the bathroom, where a series of splats and splashes witnessed to the fulfilment of her daily chore. Then a flush and the slow dribble of the cistern refilling.

The three traipsed to the back door, where Gran watched the kids at play from her folding chair. "Maeve," said Ciaran, "the three of us are after finding some food. Not sure when we'll be back."

The old woman eyed him. "Another of yer hare-brained schemes, eh, lad? Well, good luck, and take care of my girls."

"Aye, don't I always?"

"Bless you, daughter," murmured the nun. Gran cackled, as always, as the "mother" was maybe half her age.

They left the house quietly, the lovers and the nun, and for a long time traversed neighbourhood after neighbourhood similar to their own, built as clustered estates and enclaves within the maze of high walls that separated them from Protestant areas.

Presently, though, they had to cross enemy lines: the guard station they sought lay beyond two streets of loyalist homes. Aileen was very glad the nun didn't look like a nun—no headgear, no crucifix or any other accoutrements. Fine, so she maybe wasn't a real nun, but right now it was safer that way.

They progressed along the first street, feeling eyes upon them. It wasn't even a matter of religion any more and had not been for a long time. It was the simple fact that the Protestants had always been British and loyal to the Crown, and the Catholics were Irish and wanted the North to unite with the Southern Republic. Now, of course, even the Brits had been here so long they could properly be called Irish as well. Religion was mostly just lip service these days and the republic and the monarchy had both been swallowed up by the World Senate. Yet old feuds ran deep. No one wanted to tear down the walls that riddled Belfast's residential areas.

They passed the block without incident and trespassed upon the next. Here, a group of men stopped their discussion and watched the newcomers in silence. They made no move, but Aileen was as frightened as she'd ever been in her life. The looming Peace Wall, and the safe, Catholic neighbourhoods beyond its aged wire-topped concrete, felt a million miles away. And these men weren't even the real opponents in today's game of subterfuge.

Ciaran stopped them before they reached the plain but well-maintained police building. Like so much of the city, it was made of ruddy brick. It looked to be several years old; one of the last structures to be built before the current Troubles had made further new development impossible. He guided them down a side street that would bring them to its rear yard.

Dusk was falling and one or two lights winked on inside the building—electricity was still available to those on Senate business although it had become a rarity elsewhere. Ciaran crooked a finger at the deep shadow of the yard, where a vague shape indicated the garbage heap. The wire fence around the space was broken in many places and had not been repaired: Senate business notwithstanding, metal was very hard to come by, and rebuilding with wood or stone was equally unthinkable.

"You stand stooge at the corner," Ciaran instructed Mother Clementine, "and you, love, come and stand just outside the fence while I go in. I'll pass you what I find."

Clementine tiptoed back to the corner and concealed herself in the shadow of a wall. Aileen followed Ciaran to the gap in the fence and waited there, watching his foray into what was surely death-penalty territory. The Senate would abide no trespassers.

With each pace, Ciaran faded more into the milky twilight. Aileen squinted and thought she could see him crouching by the pile of waste. In a moment he straightened and hurried back. He shoved several loaves of heavy oat bread at Aileen. "Here, stack these up for Tangerine to carry."

He slipped away again. Aileen shucked off one of her shirts, many-layered for warmth, and arranged the precious cargo in it. Sure, the bread was old, and some of it was discoloured or smelled strange, but it was better than anything they'd seen in weeks.

Ciaran returned with another load, which he dumped at his wife's feet: the discarded outer leaves of cabbages, some bruised turnips, green potatoes. She reached to hold him but he was gone once more before she could grasp even his sleeve.

Something moved in her peripheral vision; she turned her head and spotted Clem waving and pointing around the corner—then she opened and closed both hands.

Ten guards? Were they coming? Aileen pointed this way and that to sign the question, but Clem wasn't looking. She peeked around her corner again, body tense, hands fisted.

Aileen trembled, waved frantically at Ciaran, but his back was turned. Why, oh, why was he taking so long? She gulped and bent to her own task. Good thing she had so many shirts on.

A light blinked on in a back room, shedding a blue glow across the trash and her red-handed husband. Slowly he rose, a burden on his back made from his own outer shirt. A figure moved in the window but did not look out. Ciaran skulked towards the gap in the fence, treading lightly. He swung out, grasped Aileen's hand and snagged the spare bundle. They sprinted for the corner, but not before Aileen heard a flush and a gurgle. She looked back as they reached Clem; the light had gone out. Aileen smirked.

Clem raised a hand to stop them from proceeding any farther. They joined her in surveying the front street. The ten or so guards she'd warned of were standing and sitting around the front steps, smoking—all but one, who sat slightly apart, head on hands. He shifted position, smoothed his hair back and revealed a row of bright lights embedded in his forehead.

Cyborg. Aileen gaped. She couldn't begin to comprehend how the implantation was accomplished—or what other horrors might be contained within his body. The light glinted strangely from his left forearm; could it be made of metal? She shivered. Imagine—the police arriving at your front door and announcing you'd been chosen for cyborg duty. Couldn't very well refuse, now, could you? They'd unemploy everyone you cared about—or worse—and end up taking you anyway. And then having to undergo the invasive personal alterations to become a Senate killing machine. Horrible.

Even from this distance, she saw the cyborg's deep breath before he stood. The broad back heaved with the volume of air intake. His head swivelled to the left, then, naturally, to the right.

"Get back!" hissed Ciaran, as he and Clem ducked into the shadow. Aileen found herself transfixed, staring into the face of death and finding only sadness there below the lighted brow. If the man could see her, he gave no indication of it, although he appeared to meet her gaze. He sighed once more, even deeper this time, then turned and said something to his comrades. Grumbles arose, but they stubbed out their cigarettes, tucked away the unused portions, and filed back into the building. The cyborg prepared to follow them but first cast a last glance at the corner where Aileen still watched.

"What is it? What's happening?" whispered Clem at her side.

The cyborg's mouth twitched. Wait—was that some sort of smile?

Then he was gone, the door shut behind him, and the street was empty.

"All clear," said Aileen. "Let's go feed the children."

Ciaran passed the third sack to Clem and they struck out towards home, picking their way among the darkened streets whose occasional lamps would soon go out at curfew. They would need to hurry now and exercise stealth when time ran out, though that was nothing new to any of them. Aileen fondled the wrapped loaves through the fabric of her shirt. The chill penetrated the remaining one on her back, but she didn't care.

This week, they would be feasting.

RUE the Night

It was half a minute to ten o'clock; the evening smoko break would be over in seconds. Shane McDermott's internal body clock told him so as precisely as if he were watching a timepiece—which, in a way, he was, as the computer components embedded throughout his flesh were attuned to universal time. He wiggled his metal digits and reflections from its shiny titanium danced on the nearby building. Heck, even his little finger probably knew what time it was.

He cast an envious gaze at the cluster of other guards, his unenhanced colleagues, and sighed. None came too close to him where he hulked on the opposite end of the wide steps. They slouched and rested, indistinct figures identified by the glowing tips of their cigarettes, scattered about near the door to the police station. He supposed he must be fairly frightening, with his instant-kill augmentations, the bullets ready inside his finger, the death-blow awaiting in his fist. If only they knew how he hated putting his enhancements to use, never mind how hard it was to get blood out of metal joints.

Alone, he sat in the circle of light emanating from the implants in his forehead. He resisted the urge to scratch at the skin around them.

It would only make the itching worse.

In the periphery of his vision, something moved. He turned his head and to his surprise and horror, locked eyes with a scrawny woman frozen at the street corner. She peered around the weathered red-brick wall of the building. Her clothing was ragged and insufficient for this cold. Her hair, tied at the nape, escaped in wisps as if she'd been running.

She gaped at him, confusion and compassion mingled on her face in a way that strongly reminded him of the last time he'd seen his mother; she'd probably never seen a cyborg before. Surely she knew the danger in being spotted this close to curfew, yet she did not duck back into the shadow.

For his part, the horror stemmed from the fact that if she was still there in twenty more seconds, he was expected to kill her.

He glanced at the officers. Apparently none of them had seen her— perhaps there was still a chance. He got to his feet, pushed through the men lounging on the entrance steps, and turned to face them. "Okeydoke, fellas, time to be back at your desks."

The guards grumbled, but did as he said, extinguishing and pocketing their half-smoked cigarettes before shuffling past him into the station. Once, he dared raise his eyes to the corner. The woman was still there, and now he made out a cloth-covered bundle in her arms. Shane's clock counted the seconds to curfew.

All at once it dawned on him why she'd been skulking around the back of the police station at such a dangerous hour. In view of the food shortage, and the relative abundance of scraps from the station's mess, the officers had begun a compost heap in the lifeless yard, thinking that perhaps the decaying organics would do a miracle on the useless soil. And now this wretch had discovered the garbage and stolen from it to feed herself.

Shane allowed himself the tiniest of smiles as he dropped his gaze and entered the building last of all. He didn't think the compost scheme had much chance of success—so far it had mostly attracted rats—and even if it did rejuvenate the earth, there would still be the problem of the seeds that refused to grow. The out-of-control terminator gene—like a contraceptive for plants—had already invaded and sterilised most of the world's edible growing things and resulted in the current shortages.

Let the woman have her slop. Rather her than the rats.

He grasped the doorhandle to shut it behind him, with a distinct clink of metal on metal. He stared at his hand, and the way the neon tubes were mirrored in its surface as he turned it this way and that. After all this time he still couldn't quite believe what they'd done to him—even though he had to spend a good deal of his off time polishing his various metal parts.

He wasn't a killer.

Not really. He killed often, of course, but he was not fervent about it as some were.

"You ready to look over tonight's route with me?" Speak of the devil. It was Fiona Butler, his one cyborg colleague in Belfast, and the most enthusiastic executioner he'd ever had the misfortune to meet.

He let his hand drop to his side, and his stomach lurched as its weight, greater than that of his natural hand, asserted itself and briefly set him off-kilter as it exerted tension on the muscles and nerve endings in the stump just below his elbow. "Aye, let's run through it now."

His mind counted out the passing of the seconds. The scavenging woman should be far away by now if she knew what was good for her, but he didn't want to let Fiona start them out on the patrol too soon, just in case. He would have to edit his memory units so that there would be no evidence of the woman at his next sync, which was…at midnight.

They approached the map. Far from attaining the Senate's claim to high technology, it was merely a collection of detailed paper street maps pasted together on the wall to create an image of the entire city. Each night someone marked off an approximate square and used a fat pen to designate a route that would cover all of the streets in that sector, with coloured pins to show the start and end. Shane hadn't ever figured out exactly whose job it was—he supposed it was one of the administrative officers. He couldn't bring himself to care, even though that person was the one who defined how he spent his nights and quite possibly, the identity of the people he would have to kill.

Completed map squares now covered most of the southwestern suburbs, but there were plenty more where they'd never walked a beat. At this rate, it would take years before they'd have to start over.

This particular base, although a few miles out from the city centre, was once advantageous in that it had been fortified by a tall wall that enclosed its yard and buildings. Now, of course, the walls had tumbled down around them and nobody had the resources for repair, least of all the distant World Senate they all worked for. Hence the ability of street strays to get right inside and pilfer the waste.

Since Shane and Fiona were the only two cyborgs in the city, they were mainly deployed on night patrol to enforce the curfew and let themselves be seen through grimy windows and gaps in curtains. If they came upon any person at large between the hours of ten and five, a single bullet from Fiona's metal finger would finish that life story forever. He was partly glad she was so forward in her duties, as it meant he bore fewer murders on his own conscience, although he was still complicit by his very existence.

When Fiona had scanned the route map into the ocular implant hidden by her shades, they prepared to leave. Shane did not possess that particular enhancement, not that he minded keeping both his own eyes. Not at all. He couldn't say the same of his hands.

They exited the building into a persistent drizzle and walked the length of the street with its enormous wall: eight feet of brick topped with eight feet of steel panels and then eight feet more of barbed wire. It was what the people had decided was necessary to stop the violence, a hundred years ago, and some said the feud still simmered beneath the surface. Never mind that the World Senate had made Irish reunification a moot point—the grudges of their great-grandfathers would not quickly crumble.

Shane felt a chill in his replaced extremities—the technicians assured him it was only ghosting on the part of the flesh limbs that had been discarded. He hated the thought that they had just been thrown away, as he'd been rather fond of his feet and his right hand: a fondness he considered to be not entirely unreasonable. Sometimes he inexplicably missed that one warty toe or the strange shape of the fingernail he'd almost sawn off as a child. He shivered, but not enough for his colleague to notice. The new parts should have been built with integrated heating, he thought for the umpteenth time. But they were made for no-nonsense functionality, not coddling of amputees.

Just as well the cyborgs' metal parts were rustproof, otherwise they'd not last long here. Ireland might be relatively warm for its latitude, due to the surrounding seas and the winds that came with them, but the same factors brought frequent dampness. Subjectively, it could be very cold even this close to summer.

Fiona guided them along the designated roads according to the plan in her heads-up display. Everywhere was still and silent except for their heavy footfalls, though Shane did spy twitches of curtains here and there. The rows of houses stood watch over roads that were thankfully empty as they should be. Shane liked to imagine the family life going on inside the homes—a life now so far out of his reach that he could only dream of it.

Sure, those families were in want of the most basic of their needs, but they were together and those who came through these times would remain together in future if things ever got better.

As for himself, Shane couldn't seriously consider the possibility of the Senate falling and there being a happy ending for cyborgs as well. His own great strength notwithstanding, sheer numbers would surely be able to overcome him once the populace were no longer threatened with punishment for such an attack. He hoped that would happen sooner rather than later, and he would not resist when they came after him, would not kill any more when he no longer had to.

The people were right to hate cyborgs. Right to hate him, with the blood that was on his hands both flesh and titanium.

He glanced up; the crescent moon was attempting to penetrate the clouds, but only glimpses of it came through the scudding haze as the ocean of vapour tufts swept by far above. He let out a deep breath, remembering how his mother used to huddle over a precious candle and read from her favourite page of a tattered Bible, the very first story in the front: "God made the sun to rule the day, and the moon to rule the night."

And the Senate made the cyborgs to rue it.

Rueful, yes, that was a good descriptor for him now, ever since he'd become this…*thing*.

In theory, cyborgs did not need as much sleep as unenhanced humans; in reality, Shane's implants caused him terrible headaches and irritation so that he thought it would be more efficient in many ways to sleep more instead. But that would mean going back, and there was no going back after augmentation. He wished he could just shut himself down and finish it, but that was a technical impossibility: his cyborg parts were hard-wired against life-ending actions. No, he'd have to find some hope to hang onto.

An image floated up into his mind: the woman at the corner again, she and her garbage-thieving ways. He was glad he'd been able to help her escape; perhaps this was worth living for. With all his heart he wished her well to whatever forces of good might be listening, then wiped her from his internal memory so she would be safe.

Immediately he noticed something was gone from his recent experience and frowned; he didn't like second-guessing himself, but had to trust that he had made a good decision not ten seconds earlier. He must have had a good reason. The sudden emptiness was no less unpleasant for all that—it must have been a happy thing he had deleted.

"So," said Shane, and paused awkwardly before continuing. The gap in his memory still niggled at him. "What was it like for you, you know, when they, er, augmented you?"

"Oh, 'twas grand," Fiona said, nostalgia creeping into her voice. "Me step-da wasna ever good to me—did a deal of harm, in fact—so I leapt at the chance to get away from him. An' they made me strong. No one can ever hurt me again."

Shane was silent a while as they clanked past yet another row of terraced houses. When he'd woken up as a cyborg, he'd felt only shrieking loss with his new metal legs, one metal forearm, and holes in his skull where lights shone out in selectable variations of white, infrared or ultraviolet, ostensibly to assist with forensic investigations although he'd done precious little of that. The physical imbalance he'd suffered, still suffered now; the removal of parts of his humanity with the lost limbs.

Words found him again at the next corner. "You weren't…sad?"

"Why should I be?" she scoffed, flapping her hands: one original, one metal. The motions of the two didn't quite match up.

It occurred to Shane that it must have been a sweet mannerism when she had a matching pair. Now, it only horrified him. He didn't know what to say, so he spoke what came to mind. "Is that so? Because I was sad."

Lame reply, boyo. No less true for all that. He attempted a puzzled frown but only got so far until his forehead implants tightened uncomfortably in his skin.

"I can't be sad." Her tone took on a steely edge. "It would ruin the electronics in my eye socket. And it'd be a bitch to clean up after." She laughed, but there was no joy in it.

They both swivelled towards a scuffle down a side street; it was only a skinny orange cat darting across between the broken-down walls of tiny front gardens that held only muck and dying weeds. The animal vanished and silence resumed as the cyborgs marched on.

Shane had cried a lot since his enhancements, behind closed doors, alone in the darkness of his windowless sleeping-room. He'd never been the weepy type before that—tough and masculine, he'd thought.

"We had no choice," he muttered mainly to himself. No one really knew on what basis the Senate chose its cyborgs—some thought good physical fitness played into it, which was ironic considering the subsequent removal of parts. Some said it was purely random, while others believed it was a punishment for some petty misdeed. Shane didn't know about that—he'd always tried to keep his head pulled in. Done his work without complaint, even when the rations first shrank. Then, that fateful twenty-second birthday, they'd sent word of his selection. When he didn't report for the scheduled amputation and reconstruction, they wrested him from the arms of his old ma on the step of her little house. They'd outright said they would shoot her then and there if he didn't submit to conversion. At that he'd ceased his resistance; he hadn't seen his mother since.

Fiona nodded. "That's true, so it is. We had no choice. But if we did…I'd have said yes." Her mouth twisted into a grin. "Hell, I'd have volunteered years before if I'd known how."

"You must have really hated your life."

"No coddin'! Hungry all the time, fending off that dirty old man, no chance at a future anyways. The day they came fer me was the happiest of my life."

This was too much for Shane. "Aw, go on and pull the other one! Ye canna be serious."

She only turned her face towards him, expression blank, her remaining eye hidden by her shades.

"Okay, partly serious?" Shane shook his head. "Sometimes I can't make you out at all."

"I'm having a good day, is all. I think about the food they give us—we'll never starve. Think of how they respect us, even the ones who made us, because they know we could destroy them in a moment if we wanted to." She sighed. "I like having that power. And the food. I want for nothing—except maybe some fun now and then."

She giggled coquettishly, and Shane reddened. Surely she wasn't suggesting…Well, maybe she was having a bit of a flirt. Certainly that might would distract them both from the unpleasant side of being turned into robots. Even if she was a cold-blooded killer…It was only what they'd made her become. Just like him.

"Hey. Race you to that Peace Wall." Shane took off, metal feet smashing into the pavement. Little pieces of concrete crumbled off with every step, but he didn't care about the old road. He strained to hear if Fiona would follow—yes, he thought he heard her steps—he slowed to give her a chance to catch up.

In a moment she zipped by him and he had to summon his very best speed. It was nothing less than exhilarating to put his muscles to full use, both his old ones and the newer augmentations in concert. Yes, he'd been forced to become a monster, but why not enjoy its good aspects? He began to see why Fiona sometimes thought it was all right, what had been done to them in the name of public order.

The two stretched out, metal fingertips extended, and both touched the wall in the same heartbeat. Fiona turned to him and held up her real hand above their heads; he high-fived it with his own, and she whooped. They let their hands linger together a few moments longer than a high-five alone would warrant. Shane couldn't read Fiona's face behind her shades, and she turned away, a pale spectre in the diffused moonlight.

There was the creak of a window from a nearby house. "Hooligans! Don't you know it's after curfew? Them cyborgs'll get you if you keep up that noise."

At this, Shane let out a guffaw.

He chanced another look at Fiona, who now appeared somehow vulnerable. A killer, but a woman, too. He moistened his lips. "Will ye let me see your face?"

Her chin jerked up and he assumed she must be staring at him. She spoke quietly. "I will, but not while we're on duty, me rig'll stop working. Another time."

"Of course." It was a simple enough request, but he was glad she hadn't said no. Disfigured as she was behind her shades, it was no small thing that she had said yes. Perhaps they weren't so different as he'd thought.

Just then, the moon sailed out from behind a cloud. Somewhere, a dog howled, the long and mournful sound carried far across the city by the night wind, and Shane thought it was the loneliest thing he'd ever heard. But for now, he was not alone, so he pitied the unseen dog and laughed again when the window slammed shut. Subtle luminescence glowed from the clammy roofs and those parts of the road that were still smooth and uncracked. Candlelight brightened the squares of curtained windows here and there, and the air had that bright, fresh scent after rain.

"Come on," said Fiona, "we've a long ways ahead of us tonight." Together, the two of them turned away from the Peace Wall and continued their patrol of the mute and suppressed streets.

With Fiona beside him, Shane thought he might make it through another night, and the day to come. As for the rueful nights after that, well, he didn't have to think about those just yet.

StRAWBERRY ÐREAMING

It is a warm summer day. Layers of wispy clouds do little to obscure the sun, for once. These temperatures are rare in Ireland—but all the more treasured for it. The air carries wondrous scents of flowering things and the promise of tree fruit in autumn: apples and pears and plums now ripening, the unborn ghosts of their nascent aromas already filling the orchard slopes.

Railway tracks border the green area, with rows of brick houses beyond. Farther still, to the north, are the tall chimneys of an industrial area nearer the city, and on the left hand looms the dark shape of the Black Mountain that overhangs western Belfast. A train rattles by, its wheels screeching, the commuters gazing with longing at the paradise that is lost to them a few seconds later. In the midst of the city the allotments bloom. Tired brick and old streets have given way to a space between the walls where determined gardeners have staked a claim and worked the land.

Even now there is a harvest of other crops, the summer vegetables and early fruit. The little girl stoops, reaches into a tangle of leaves, and twists a strawberry from its socket with a pleasing *pop*. Her sharp eyes watch to confirm what her fingers have already told her. When she brings it out into view, it is intensely scarlet and fills the palm of her small hand, a thing of beauty with a drop of juice barely clinging on at the recently detached summit. She breathes its essence, warm and ripe, a storehouse of sunshine and satiety, the secure anticipation of how it is going to feel on her tongue as she savours it and her tastebuds explode with simple happiness.

She bites into it, but something is wrong. It's not really there. Her mouth is vacant, no matter how she tongues it.

"Mariah!" The whisper infiltrating her mind, but she must resist, hiding away in her soul's secret place.

A spark of the synapses. Realisation slowly dawning on her...

"Wake up! We'll be late."

She groaned. *Yes, something is very wrong.* Very wrong with the entire world, where nothing grew any more, least of all a strawberry. She defied alertness a moment longer, trying in vain to recapture the aroma of that fruit, but the effort only awakened her brain even more. She was not a little girl, she was not in the allotments, and the allotments didn't look like that any more.

There was a tug at her shoulder and she finally came upright with a grunt and shook her dazed head to clear it of sleep. She had been dozing in the cafeteria, face smushed on forearms with her nose in the gap, leaning on the table. The cafeteria might not be worthy of the name these days, but dining tables made passable headrests for snatching a few winks.

Liam shook her shoulder again, peering at her from under his thatch of red hair. "Wakey-wakey. You trying to get us in trouble?"

She surveyed the empty room with its rows of benches. Only young Jonesy was visible, cleaning up on the other side of the servery hatch. Poor kid, by rights he ought to be growing more, but who could grow in times like these? She smiled at the painfully skinny boy and blinked hard.

Unsteadily she got to her feet, refusing Liam's proffered hand. He continued to hover, though she didn't want his support. A thought formed itself, that Liam didn't have to get himself in trouble—why was it always "us" with him anyway—but a glance at his earnest eyes told her it was pointless. He was inexplicably determined to stick by her.

Together they strode out of the eatery and across the narrow gap between buildings, into their workplace. Just before they stepped inside, a stray ray of sunshine burst through the clouds as a puff of wind caressed them.

Mariah sighed. The rest of her dream might have been a fairytale, but the weather was a perfect match. Such a beautiful day to be stuck in the "office".

It barely fit the definition at all. Only a tin-roofed concrete-block shed with a few ramshackle old computers and desks that had all been repaired so many times they were hardly recognisable. Cracked monitors still served above dusty processor towers whose fans sounded like the death-rattle. Broken desk legs had been replaced or simply shored up with whatever stick-like item had been to hand. Years of rain had stained the porous floor just left of Mariah's yet-unbroken chair that she was very glad of, beneath a rusty spot in the roof. She was well-practised in avoiding its trajectory on wet days—and also well-practised in staring at the hole, analysing its spread from season to season. Through the worst of last winter she had finally placed a bucket on the floor to catch the drips, but one day she'd forgotten to take it home and in the morning it had vanished. She didn't have another.

Despite all this, it was the Northern Department of Farming Statistics, and they were bonded to it for a plate of porridge each noon. Unless of course the Senate authorities saw fit to transfer them somewhere else, which might happen at any time.

This wasn't such a bad place to work, was esteemed and sought-after because it did not involve physical labour in the grain processing plants or few remaining fertile fields. People joked that office workers would become fat and lazy.

Mariah knew the reality was different: nobody could be fat on these rations.

The department manager raised her eyebrows when they entered the building, and she tapped her bare wrist. Mariah made for her desk, trying to look contrite. They wouldn't get in trouble—the manager knew Mariah and Liam were her most conscientious workers, and they'd still get much more done than anyone else even if a few minutes were shaved off their time.

Giggling emanated from halfway along the room. It was Kitty and Elsbeth, tittering behind their hands and peering over them at the latecomers. Mariah didn't know why they were tolerated when they did so little work and often caused distractions. Silly girls, heads full of fluff, too naïve for her to hold anything against them.

Liam slid into his chair nearby. "Were you dreaming something nice, then?"

Mariah fiddled a moment with her mouse and used it to pull up a new harvest report for checking and processing. "Aye, that I was. Do you remember the allotments?"

"Not really. That was a bit before my time, and I woulda thought a bit before yours as well."

"I can't have been more than three or four. I guess it just made such a huge impression on me that I never forgot it." She closed her eyes and saw it spread out before her again, larger than life: the sunshine, the fruit trees, the humps of leaf-swamped dirt in the strawberry patch. "It was my uncle's allotment. I only went there once or twice. He grew all kinds of things…but I remember the strawberries. They were massive and sweet and they tasted like heaven."

"I woulda liked to know what that was like." Liam's voice grew wistful. "Before it all died out."

There was the scrape of a chair in the corner, and both Mariah and Liam shot their attention to their screens.

"Enough with the chatter, you two," called the boss, without bothering to get up. This pronouncement was followed by hushed laughter from Kitty. Elsbeth only stared openly at Mariah, her glee evident. Mariah shot her a withering glare, to which Elsbeth poked out her tongue. Mariah shook her head.

For a while Mariah dedicated herself to entering the reported figures for Farm E in County Down. The name was meaningless to her, but it was the only official designation and might equally have been in Donaghadee or Downpatrick. This farm had in any case just scraped into the "acceptable" bracket of standard results once again. Of course all the brackets had been redefined three times last year, and what had been labelled insufficient then might have passed now.

There was no reason to it, no reason to say this farm was doing okay when it clearly wasn't. Mariah could only guess that the authorities wanted to be able to assure the public that everything was going fine, to pre-empt unrest and looting.

Only the human drones in Statistics knew the full truth.

This line of thinking could only occupy Mariah's mind for so long before she had to drop it to avoid spiralling into total negativity. Topics other than food—and the lack thereof—were hard to come by. Mariah's mind filled once more with the memory of her uncle's garden and the fruit that tasted of real life, real nutrition, she knew that now. It was a wonder people still found the strength to stand when mostly all they got to eat was a bit of oats and maybe some wild greens, if the rare hardy weeds that still grew could even be counted as sustenance.

She almost gagged at the thought of the dandelion leaves she'd had to eat last night: sour, tough and nigh on unchewable even when boiled for a full half hour, but they did stop a stomach from rumbling too much. If she or Da could find some, tonight's dinner would be the same again. Or it might be nothing at all. She'd slept hungry more times than she cared to enumerate.

Mariah closed her eyes for a moment to imagine that perfect strawberry. She nodded once, rallied, then sagged. It was there before her in her mind's eye, a luscious red, pocked with non-terminating seeds, and the smell—oh, that aroma would move mountains, she was sure of it. If she could just eat this solitary one, she wouldn't need any dinner. Then the fruit was in her hand and she was raising it up to her face. Her mouth opened.

Her teeth clacked shut on nothing.

The sound reverberated inside her skull and jolted her upright in the chair. She shot a glance around the room to see if anyone had noticed.

Liam caught her eye and grinned. She looked away; he didn't matter. Well, it wasn't that he didn't matter—it was more that it didn't matter if he was the one who caught her snoozing.

Then, laughter. *Oh—botheration.* Mariah snuck a look towards Elsbeth and found her head to head with Kitty as they whispered in each other's ears, clacked their teeth together and burst into fresh giggles. Mariah felt mutinous. She didn't mind the work, but the taunting was almost too much for any reasonable soul to bear. What was this, primary school? Well, those girls were probably only in their mid-teens and had been drafted just like young Jonesy, just like everyone in this dratted place. She brushed off her anger. It would only make her more hungry as soon as lunch wore off.

Her focus drifted in and out through the interminable afternoon. As quitting time approached, she checked the minutes on her computer again and again. Finally the display ticked over to six o'clock, the hour she'd spent all day waiting for.

As she stood and gathered her things and pulled on her well-worn cap and jacket, she reminisced again about the once-glorious allotment. She'd gone back a few years ago to sate her curiosity and see if the soil could be salvaged, but without decaying plant matter it had turned to soulless muck.

Instead of that juicy strawberry, the image that now pressed itself onto her mind was that of the same garden patch—but now dead and with no hope of producing anything resembling a crop. She'd wept as she'd stood in the wasteland of swiftly eroding mud between the railway tracks, the once-green hills now brown in the distance, the houses falling into disrepair, the cold, damp wind whipping at her hair and clothes. She'd weep again now if she wasn't careful; she gulped hard and got herself under control. Hoping for better from the allotments after the onset of the viral terminator gene had been a pie-in-the-sky idea anyway.

The day had started to cool towards evening, although the sun wouldn't set until some time after the ten o'clock curfew. Mariah did up the buttons on her patched and quilted coat: sure it looked funny, but it kept her warm through a good part of the year. Winter was another story, but it was a long way off. She'd have to add another layer of patchwork to the inside before then, and some extra padding if she could get hold of it.

The office workers moved in a gaggle towards the door. "Just a moment," said the boss, and heads turned towards her. "Kitty and Elsbeth. A word, if you don't mind."

In the alley, Mariah unlocked her bike from the rail fence and looked around for Liam. He seemed to have disappeared—his wheels were still here so he couldn't be far away. Mariah caught herself and smiled faintly. He'd been behaving like a lovesick puppy and while she'd gotten used to having him around all the time and being so attentive through the working day, she wasn't sure she had the sort of feelings he obviously had for her. There were far worse options, to be sure. Perhaps she'd end up with him after all…If so, she'd try to talk him out of having children, bringing them into such a messed-up world where even their ma and da wouldn't be certain of feeding them properly each day. Look at how poor Jonesy was suffering. No, she didn't want her child to live like that, a wage-slave before his ninth birthday, and still not enough to eat.

She blinked and shook her head. That was clearly too far for her mind to wander, where Liam was concerned. She was firmly decided that nothing could come of it, not with the way the world was. Still, against her better judgement, she delayed swinging aboard to head home, pretending to check the tyre while her other workmates said their farewells and left.

Sure enough, a short while later came the pounding of feet. Liam skidded round the corner of the building. "Oh good, you're still here." He approached, one fist closed, but not tightly. "Uh, here. This is for you."

At his gesture she opened her palm and stretched it out. He loosened his fingers, dropping a single strawberry into her hand. It was the size of her thumbnail, fringed with pale green beneath its crown of leaves—but a strawberry!

Aghast with delight, she met his gaze. "How—where did you get this?"

Liam pointed his thumb back over his shoulder. "Found it in one of the alleys." He stuck his hands in the pockets of his ragged jeans and dipped his head, clearly pleased at her joy.

Mariah nodded. She wouldn't ask him to reveal more than that. Such secrets were personal, especially since the plant would likely keep growing and produce more fruit if it had been lucky enough to root itself into living, nutrient-holding soil. Liam needed to keep that to himself.

She lifted the berry to her face—so much like she'd been dreaming of—and inhaled deeply. The scent was faint but unmistakable. She closed her eyes a moment and felt herself transported back in time. Then the facts slapped her back to the present.

Liam. Gave her a gift. A most precious possession. That must really mean…No, no. She couldn't let him do this. "Liam, don't, this is too much." She looked up from the tiny fruit into his crestfallen face.

Slowly he reached out with both hands and closed her fingers over it. "I want you to have it. Really."

Something within her stirred at his touch, an unexpected awakening. The dream was no longer important. If Mariah accepted this gift, she'd be encouraging Liam in his feelings for her. But he wasn't letting her open her hand. He just stared at her with those burning emerald eyes. How could the colour green burn? She didn't know, but she did know it was the exact colour of those lush strawberry leaves from long ago.

When he finally broke contact, he grabbed his bike and sailed off before she could stop him. He didn't look back, but stood up on his pedals and gave it his best speed, swiftly vanishing from sight around the corner.

"Liam," she called, but he was gone. She stood alone in the street, clutching a strawberry that must be protected at all costs. If it had been growing wild, its seeds might even be viable. Mariah looked down at it. What had the world come to, that such a small thing should carry such significance? It even served as proof irrevocable of a young man's love.

She would deal with Liam later. Somehow. For now, she had strawberry seeds to nurture, once she got them to a safe place and figured out how best to coax them into germination. It wouldn't be easy, but she had to try. *Had* to.

Two late leavers came giggling out of the office. Great. Just her luck: Elsbeth and Kitty, of course. Perhaps the boss had been lecturing them.

They stopped and looked Mariah up and down with great exaggeration, then traipsed away down the alley. Their whispers and peals of childish laughter assured her they were unlikely to be an actual threat to this great treasure with which she'd been entrusted, as well as unlikely to have listened to anything the boss had said, but she was still glad the strawberry was well hidden in her cupped hand. Who knew what sort of a big deal the young troublemakers would have made out of it.

When they were well out of sight, she wrapped it in a clean hanky and tucked it into a section of her bag where it couldn't be damaged.

Taking care to ensure it kept its safe position, she mounted and rode away—slowly at first, then gathering speed. The lowering sun for a second turned even the ugly industrial area to gold, and Mariah's solitary figure with it.

callum's alley

Eight-year-old Callum Jones scrubbed his rag harder on the chipped formica of the servery counter and cast another glance through the hatch. Two diners remained in the cafeteria; they were past due back at their jobs by now, so Callum waited, hoping he wouldn't get in trouble for tardiness so clearly not his own. The large room echoed with the lilt of their soft conversation, but they were too far away for him to make out any words.

It was Mariah, exhaustion writ plain on her features, and Liam, stammering, something on his mind perhaps. Callum liked them—they called him Jonesy and treated him like a little brother. He had a brother already, true enough, but he had been assigned to work on a farm somewhere in the far reaches of County Down, and Callum hadn't seen him for maybe three years. It was hard to remember his brother's face when he had been so little himself at the time.

Callum allowed his mind to drift to a happier memory: this morning, when he'd left home early so as to have time to walk by the river and let the wind blow in his face. It made him feel alive; he pined all through the workdays for those moments on the banks each morning and afternoon. If it was warm enough he'd dip his feet in the

41

mostly-icy water or even dive completely under. His mother complained when he came home in wet clothes, so he mooched around to let them dry before he arrived back in his own street. She didn't like him leaving so early, but he'd made a habit of it now, and it had become his normal schedule as far as the family knew.

Today it had been particularly beautiful; he'd swung out of his little front gate and dashed along the road, glancing back to see his father shaking his head at the enthusiasm. It was not enthusiasm for work, however. He'd arrived at the water's edge, torn off his ramshackle old shoes, and plunged in up to his knees, careful to hoist the hems of his shorts out of reach of the water. The coolness felt so good on his skin, as if he absorbed it for nutrition, though he knew this was impossible.

He'd stayed and paddled until the very last minute, then dashed up the bank and the crumbling concrete stairs to the promenade. Finding a patch of grass, he hurriedly wiped the sand off his feet as best he could and crammed his shoes back on before setting off at high speed towards his place of work. He'd only just avoided a telling-off from his boss, and had grabbed the tools of his trade to start cooking lunch even before he caught his breath. Then he'd served all of the meals, precisely measured, and then he'd finally had the chance to gulp down his own small ration.

Now, when Liam and Mariah were gone, he would go and wipe down the tables, not that there was ever any real mess to clean up. Mariah always liked to sit in the far corner; she'd assured him it wasn't to get away from him. When the medics came with new compulsory vaccination shots, they always got the folks near the door first of all, and as much as Mariah hated needles, she liked to have the extra time to prepare herself for the ordeal.

People were so hungry he'd seen them lick spills off the tables and benches, though not the floor. That tragedy had only occurred once that he knew of. He hadn't seen the sad event but he did find the mess under a table and furtively snuck most of it into his own mouth, dust and all. This contributed to a considerable lessening of the tragic element for himself personally. He fondly remembered how his stomach had felt after the extra meal: warm and more satisfied than any other time he could remember. Ever since then, he'd been particularly careful to mop the floor each morning so that it would definitely be clean enough to eat off. But there had been no more spillages.

Callum and his parents had been happy about his work assignment, as it might have meant more food—first for him and then maybe scraps to take home, but he had not been so lucky. His ration of oat porridge was the same as any other child's and the diners were certainly not in the habit of leaving any leftovers. His ma and da had hidden him a long time; children were supposed to start being useful at six but hardly anyone let their kids work so soon. He didn't see his friends much any more since they'd all started working—even the ones who lived nearby. Long hours exhausted them and nobody played in the street of an evening as they used to when they were younger, tossing and catching, chasing about and shrieking in the innocent freedom of childhood.

He surveyed the dining hall again. Mariah had fallen asleep, her head on the table, and Liam approached her carefully, hissing wakey-wakey noises. Then he shook her shoulder, but so gently, as if she was a china doll that might shatter at his touch. Eventually Mariah raised her head, shook herself, and struggled to her feet. She caught Callum's eye and bestowed an empathetic smile before dragging out of the room in Liam's wake. He'd heard their boss was lenient with those two because they were particularly efficient, so maybe they wouldn't cop any flak.

"Hey, kid," called Magnus from the other end of the room. "Did you finish cleaning yet?"

Callum ran the rag over the servery counter one more time while he considered his answer. He wished Magnus would use his name instead of calling him "kid." But Magnus wasn't a bad boss, just short-tempered at times. He had no reason to be angry—he had the look of a well-fed man, so perhaps he had figured out a way to pilfer more than his fair share of the cafeteria supplies. Callum pressed his lips together and then replied in a studiously polite tone, "No, sir, there was people still out there."

"Slackers, eh?" Magnus appeared beside him and surveyed the dining room. "Well, they're gone, so get to it."

Callum slunk with his bucket to the alley door and opened it with one hand. It was old, in need of grease, and the wood hung oddly in its frame so that it jammed on the floor, having formed a deep, arced groove in the worn linoleum. Yet practice had bestowed finesse and he forced it to let him pass.

Outside, he paused for a moment to inhale the freshness. A breeze from the north brought salt air from the docklands not too far distant. A seagull's cry reached him on the wind. How he longed to run there and plunge into the early summer sea just beyond the river's mouth. But he could not. He must complete his allotted hours or forfeit tomorrow's only meal.

With a sigh, he dumped the dirty water from his bucket into the gutter between the run-down brick buildings. He was well-practised at this also, so that it made the largest possible splash. A kid had to have *some* fun, right? He watched the resulting splatter gleefully and was about to trudge back inside when a movement caught his eye.

There, behind the dumpster—what could it be? Something white shifted in the shadow; white, but partly grey too, so that only odd, unrecognisable shapes were clear.

He glanced behind him at the kitchen door. Didn't want to get in trouble, but this was just too curious to ignore. Cautiously he set down the empty bucket and advanced on silent feet. The thing shrank back, so that Callum had to squat on hands and knees to peer into the small space.

Just a little farther…there.

Callum came face to face with a terrified white and grey kitten. She mewed at him, and the sound almost broke his heart. He extended a hand, slowly, as she watched with the widest golden eyes he'd ever seen on a creature so tiny.

She sniffed his fingers, then butted her head into his palm and stepped out into the light.

"Oh, yer a skinny wee 'un, so you are." Callum ran his hand down her bony spine. Nobody fed cats these days, they had to make do with what small wildlife they could catch. But this kitten was surely too young to know how. He wondered what had happened to her mother.

He slid his fingers under her belly and lifted her up; she did not squirm, and he cradled her to his chest. Immediately a loud rumbling purr shook her body from top to toe and her little claws kneaded Callum's threadbare flannel shirt. He inspected her white paws and grey ears, grey tail and splotches over her back and sides.

"We'll have to see about getting you a bite to eat," he muttered, knowing as he said it that such a task was nigh impossible. Tomorrow, he would save part of his own food, but for now, everything edible in the kitchen was securely under lock and key, and the key securely in the grip of Magnus.

Callum looked around. Magnus would be searching for him in seconds if he didn't get back to work quick smart. "Here, let's find you a bed." Pressing the creature to him with one hand, he reached into the dumpster and retrieved a dry cardboard box. He placed it in the gap behind the large bin, so that it was practically out of sight.

The kitten stiffened in his arms. Callum swung around, thinking Magnus had caught him—but it was only a dog that had snuck up behind him. Unlike many dogs it did not want to chase the cat; it merely sat some distance away, tongue lolling in a smile. Callum eyed the animal while grasping the one he held even tighter. The dog was not large, nor small, nor any particular breed, just some sort of brown with floppy ears and grey patches. The little cat wriggled and tucked her head into the crook of Callum's elbow—so helpless, he determined to save her life any way he could.

Callum took a firm, menacing step towards the dog. "Go on home, then."

The dog departed regretfully, or at least Callum thought so. He regretted sending him away as well, because he might have been a friend to him, but right now the kitten needed him more. With one last backwards glance the dog trotted out of sight at the end of the alley.

Callum clutched the kitten a second longer, and then conveyed her into the box he'd hidden safely behind the dumpster. She clung to him, didn't want to let go; gently he released each delicate claw from his clothing and settled her into the hideout. Her purr grew quieter, but did not altogether stop.

He petted her once more, retrieved his bucket, and filled it with clean water from the tap by the door. Fetching a fresh rag, he zipped into the dining hall and set to his task with energy, if not exactly with a will.

Callum had never known any life where food was plentiful, but his parents talked about the good old days all the time. He wondered what it would be like to eat whenever he was hungry. Still, his ma and da had managed to feed him once most days, whether by scrounging for greens or by giving up some of their own earned meal.

He worked his way down one table and up the next, covering the room in long zig-zags. His thoughts kept drifting back to the baby cat in the alley, and he hoped she would have a good life. She certainly would if he could do anything about it. Oats from his own ration were not proper food for cats, he was fairly sure of that, but maybe he could ask his father to help him cobble together some mouse traps around their tiny house. Then he could bring meat for the young one—or better yet, take her home with him and feed her there.

The family's assigned single-story terraced house might be humble, but they'd made it as comfortable as they could. Callum slept in the living room on an old broken-down settee while his parents shared the one small bedroom. He thought it was all right, though he'd never lived anywhere different.

For now, everything was quiet in the cafeteria; there was no sound except for the soft swish of his rag on old wood and the drip of water when he rinsed it and squeezed it out.

He rounded the last table in the far corner of the room and stopped short, gaping, at the sight of a tidy pile of cold porridge on the bench, well hidden from the view of the kitchen. He shot a glance to the hatch anyway to make sure, but Magnus had already slid the shutters closed.

Callum knelt before the treasure, hesitating only a moment before dipping his head to slurp it straight from the wooden bench. He closed his eyes and swallowed—such a satisfying gulp—then regarded the remainder, a bit more than half a mouthful. He was about to suction it up too, when he remembered the hungry kitten outside. This might just be enough to fill her stomach and tide her over until he could trap some better food for her. Callum wanted this last small bite very much, but he heard the high-pitched meows once more in his mind.

Quickly he finished wiping the rest of the final table, then returned and used the side of one hand to scrape the food into his open left palm. He licked his right hand clean, swiped the rag over the bench where the porridge had been, and snuck back towards the kitchen.

Callum waited by the door, listening, his left hand closed over the food, but not so tightly that it would squeeze out. All was quiet, so perhaps Magnus was in the storeroom. Callum backed himself in through the swing door and turned around, almost dropping his burdens when he came face to face with Magnus stomping to meet him.

"There y'are. What's taking ye so long, then?" The fat man's shaggy eyebrows almost met in his frown. "I need you to weigh tomorrow's ration."

"Aye, boss. I'll just go an' empty this out." He tilted his head at the bucket in his right hand. His left he kept behind his back.

Magnus nodded once and lumbered on to whatever important task a kitchen manager had next.

Callum quaked, but pushed on. If discovered, he'd likely be accused of stealing, no matter how he insisted it was a spill. He pushed down on the doorhandle with his elbow—a difficult ambition, considering its stiffness, but he refused to fail. He dragged the bucket outside, careful not to use or even move his left hand.

The little cat was nowhere in sight, not even in the box he'd prepared for her. "Here, kitty, kitty," Callum called softly. He had no time to spare—Magnus would want him immediately.

Wind whistled down the alley, bringing a few splashes of rain. The box faced north; perhaps the kitten had sought a more adequate shelter from the weather. He abandoned the bucket and grabbed the box, intending to place it somewhere less open.

The gap at the south end of the dumpster appeared favourable. But there was still no sign of his friend. Time grew shorter still.

A scuffle interrupted his increasing panic and the tiny shape scrambled out from under the dumpster itself. "Meow," she said, and approached, sniffing the air.

Callum opened his hand and spread the porridge into the box, which he wedged into its new spot, then stepped back to allow some space. The youngster neared it slowly, sniffed the entire mess from end to end, and slurped up a bite. Callum licked the last remains of the windfall from his hand as he watched.

Inside, Magnus yelled, and Callum hurried to empty his bucket well away from the kitten and her meal. He hesitated another moment before going in to face his fate. "You 'n' me, we'll be chums, eh? Alley cat." There was no reaction, but Callum smiled anyway. The cat's obvious enjoyment was answer enough. "Alley, that's your name, so it is."

Callum slipped inside, shut the door, and stowed the bucket in its place.

Magnus loomed over him, red-faced. He opened his mouth wide. "Boy, you've been a right slacker today. Takin' so long over your work. Should be ashamed of yerself."

Callum cringed at the verbal onslaught, but said nothing. There was no point. But he trembled a little at the thought that he might lose his job and his secure meal each workday.

"Hmph." Magnus grimaced. "Stay an extra hour every day this week and I'll say no more of it if you work hard. I won't have a lazybones in my kitchen. Now go get that measuring cup, and no dallying!"

Weariness slid into Callum's bones at the thought of the extra work. He wouldn't have time to stop by the river on his way home, not even briefly. No doubt Magnus would have him scrub every inch of the place over and over again. At least he still had his job, he consoled himself ineffectively as his hand sought the government-mandated oat ration cup from its hook on the wall.

But it wasn't so bad—because at long last, he might have a friend to play with again. The door to the dining hall stood ajar; from this angle he was now certain that the extra porridge had been a gift from Mariah.

The corners of his mouth twitched upwards again and gripped the half-cup measure. He stepped across the decrepit kitchen towards the storeroom where Magnus waited with the key.

"Alley," he whispered, and even in the midst of his hungry, bleak life, his heart grew warm.

ONE MAN'S WORK

Ellis Flanegan cast a glance at the silent buzzer above the exit of the processing hall. The cavernous room echoed with the clank of machines and the attempted banter of tired workers, these monotonous sounds bouncing back from the crumbling concrete brickwork and brown-tinged roof of corrugated iron. Broad and expansive as it was, it still felt like a prison. Ellis certainly considered it to be such.

Lunchtime must surely be soon, but it wasn't yet, so he ruefully returned his attention to the aging grain mill before him—meeting Dougie's glance on the way. His colleague grimaced, and Ellis knew why.

Today his stomach was somehow emptier than usual and he grumbled unintelligible cusses to himself, even as his hands reached for the next motions in his repeated cycle of work. Ellis filled the milling stone again with wheat grain, turned it the required three times with the crank handle (any more would remove too much bran, which was filling if not exactly nutritious), swept the fan across to uplift the chaff, and opened a hatch to send the softened grain to the central conveyor chute that filled the bags to load in closely guarded trucks that would

51

deliver food to the counties of Antrim and Down and maybe even beyond.

A violent tremor went through Ellis' stomach and he laid a hand on it for a moment to ease the pang, the movement garnering a sympathetic look from the woman beside him. She was new here, and terrified to make some misstep and lose the position; her name was Jasmine if he remembered rightly. His thoughts weren't really on her, however. He was sunk into his favourite daydream—a memory, really, of his wife's happy presence and her cooking in the days before the shortage. She'd make meat pies and sausage omelettes, gravy stews and airy scones. He could almost smell it all if he imagined hard enough.

Together they'd taken such joy in giving good things to their children—first Darian, then Mariah. Then, seven years ago, everything had changed: the corporations took over the government, requisitioned the workforce, then changed the pay from money to food. And none too much of that, either.

"Pssst." It was Jasmine, waking him from his reverie. He looked down—damn it, he'd been grinding the wheat too long and it lay there all but white and naked. Carefully he fanned away some of the chaff, but not all, or the white would show brightly and get him in trouble.

But Jasmine wasn't done yet. She raised the back of her hand to him and waggled her fingers. A tiny emerald-coloured stone glinted there in a knotwork setting of cheap silver. "Can I interest ye in a ring, Ellis?"

"Yer wedding ring? What fer?"

"Nice fella like you needs a present for his lady."

Ellis' horror must have shown on his face. The bottom fell out of his world...no, it was only a memory. His eyes lost their focus and threatened wateriness as he relived it.

Jasmine winced. "I'm sorry. I need to feed my wains."

Ellis sighed. She didn't know. "My wife...my wife died six years ago." And he didn't have anything to trade, either, assuming she wanted food. He glanced at the ring—it reminded him of the baubles sold in tourist shops when he was a wee fella.

Jasmine looked stricken. Ellis spoke no more but concentrated on doing his task correctly. Before the World Senate takeover, his Amy would have survived that fever, there would have been doctors and medicines to save her life. All the medics had vanished—well, except for the lackeys who came around with the vaccine shots every other week or so—ostensibly the rest were in Senate scientific research centres to help find a biological solution to the lack of plant growth. So Amy had died, leaving Ellis with two teens angry at the world—and rightfully so. He was angry too. The three of them had clung even closer together and their maturity had amazed him.

Soon after, tragedy had struck again when Senate guards had arrived one evening to take Darian to a workcamp in Antrim. He was promised better rations, and he kept a brave face, only burying his tears in his dog's long fur. His last instruction as he'd pushed the collie towards his sister: "Take care of her."

People didn't come back from the camps, Ellis knew that. Jemima was a very old dog now but he still held out an impossible hope that she would see her master again.

Ellis let his gaze drift across the factory floor. At every stage of the procedure were men and women in well-worn clothes, pulling levers, opening or sealing bags, carrying them outside. Supervisors wandered around ensuring nobody snuck any handfuls of the precious food, and they'd all be frisked again upon leaving. It wasn't enough to deter some people; just last week some newbie had been caught, her overlarge boots filled with wheat around her dainty feet. "Have pity on my children," she'd sobbed. That's what they all said. It made no difference—the guards had taken her away and no one had seen her since. Ellis hoped she "only" lost her job, though even that was a drastic punishment these days. Worst case, they might have sent her to a workcamp and left the children to fend for themselves unless their da was still around, or a relative or neighbour consented to take them in and share their own meagre supplies.

Workcamp…Ellis sighed. His thoughts zapped back to his son. He claimed to have lost count of the years, but he knew to the day how long they'd been parted. There was no warning, no chance to hide, no option of choosing to go or stay. The guards had simply announced their intentions, and waited impatiently while Darian packed a small bag and said his hasty goodbyes. He had tried to reassure hos ol' Da that it was for the best, that he would get good food there in exchange for his work. But there were tears in his eyes even as Ellis hugged him for the last time and agreed, for the benefit of the watching guards: "Yes, son. Great food."

Voices roused him once more and he was pleased to see he hadn't overdone the current batch. He dropped it down the chute and refilled the stone while trying to pinpoint the conversation he'd heard.

"I'll take it," said Dougie at his side.

Jasmine, on his other side, blinked and gulped. "What you got to trade, then?"

"Not now." Dougie nodded at one of the supervisors approaching. "We'll talk later, but I'll give you a good price for it."

"For the sake of the children," whispered Jasmine, a trace of her recently doomed colleague's sentiment in her tone.

Children. Ellis was so proud of his two, even though Darian was as good as lost to him. In the face of all they had survived, Mariah had only become more kind, and wise beyond her years. Even just the other night on their walk, they'd come across a drunk mistreating his dog. Mariah had waded right in and given him a proper telling-off, told the lout in no uncertain terms to treat the animal better.

Across the hall, an anomaly interrupted the identical, repeated movements of the workers. Ellis squinted. If he had seen it so easily, then there was going to be trouble. He watched carefully as he ground his wheat, paused to refill, scanned the line of workers again.

Yes. There it was. Ellis' heart sank.

A young man had slipped a handful of precious grain into his mouth. After several seconds his Adam's apple moved up and down.

The unground wheat would be all but indigestible. Perhaps the fellow realised this, because after he ground his next batch, his hand scooped from the stone before he sent the rest down the chute. How could he dare to be so brazen? It was not dark in the hall. He was gambling on the inattention of the supervisors, but if he kept up like this, someone would see him sooner rather than later.

Ellis stared, hoping he'd feel himself observed and give up. No such luck. When the man's hand came away from his face, it actually left traces of white from the milled wheat. Ellis shook his head. The man swallowed again. He must have doubled his lunch by now, albeit a lunch that felt somewhat overdue.

More movement in the corner of his eye. Ellis glanced to the far end of the hall, where a supervisor had frozen like a statue in a thinking pose, one arm folded and the other hand on her chin. Was she watching the violator? Ellis thought she might be.

He returned his attention to the young man and tried to catch his eye without making himself more noticeable in the process—not an easy task. "Dammit, look over here!" he muttered.

The man couldn't have heard him across the noisy workspace, but his timing was uncanny: he turned and gazed straight at Ellis just as he scooped more grain from the stone.

Ellis shook his head as hard as he could and then tilted it towards the supervisor. Both Ellis and the young man glanced that way just as the supervisor tapped a guard on the shoulder and pointed down the line. The guard fetched another guard and both set off towards the youngster, who dropped his handful and hurriedly swiped his hand on his pants in an attempt to remove the incriminating evidence. He shook visibly as he reached to empty the processed grain and refill it; he shuddered as he turned the crank.

Once.

Twice.

The guards gripped him by the upper arms and all but carried him away from his station. He met Ellis' gaze once more, anguish and resignation writ across his face. Ellis sent him as much sympathy as he could; a young chap like that would no doubt go straight to a workcamp. Just like Darian. Ellis wished he could do something, but any movement he made to stand by the young man would only get both of them in trouble, and there was no sense in that.

Whispers flew around the room as other workers noticed what was happening. An older woman in the processing line screamed and deserted her post. She ran to the youngster and tried to pull him away, but the guards didn't loosen their grip.

"He's my son! Please, take me instead."

One of the guards laughed. "Lady, it weren't you as stole Senate property. Besides, who'd send you to hard labour? Ye'd be dead in a month."

"You're more use here," said the other. "Now get back to work before we cut your rations."

They dragged the boy off—Ellis saw now that he couldn't be much older than mid-teens—while his mother wailed behind him. Nearby workers reached out to hold her; the supervisors turned a blind eye for a moment.

The door slammed and the woman slumped, then turned and trudged back to her station. She seized the crank handle. Her sobs were muffled by her grinding millstone; the sound fell into an unnatural silence and Ellis realised everyone had stopped what they were doing.

"All right, back to work," called a supervisor from somewhere, and the racket started back up along with some hushed chit-chat, but the mood was subdued and Ellis preferred to lose himself in daydreams of better times while still making sure he didn't grind any of his batches too long.

At length, the buzzer sounded and the workers stepped away from their places. Ellis filed out of the hall with the rest, submitted unwillingly to the pat-down, and was about to turn left to go to the dining room when he noticed everyone else was headed the other way, chattering in soft voices. He stood still in the shadows for a moment as they swirled past him into the bright evening sunshine. How could he lose track of half a day like that? He'd been so sure it was lunchtime he'd been waiting for, not knock-off. Well, he wasn't a young man any more.

He was about to head out himself when whispers stopped him in his tracks. Dougie and Jasmine huddled together just inside the door; they would not be able to see him where he stood in the dark, before the blinding line of light cut across the dusty hallway. Not that they would have minded terribly much if he caught them—he would never spill the beans—but he didn't wish to disturb their dealings even though every word came to him clear as day. He froze in place and listened.

"I thought you said you had something to trade?" Jasmine pleaded.

Dougie cast a glance about him. "I will, tomorrow, I tell ya."

"You better not be filchin' it from here. We all saw how quickly they caught that poor boy."

"No, no. Somewhere else. But not till tomorrow."

"Then tomorrow is when you get the ring."

"Ye dinna understand. I have to use the ring to trade fer the food."

"Who with? I'll go to them myself."

"No can do. Have to keep the contact under wraps."

Jasmine's eyes went wide. "Someone on the inside, then."

Dougie pressed his lips together. "Not a word to anyone, d'ya hear?" He sighed. "Look, it has to be me who trades with him. Surely you understand that."

"Aye, but what if I never get the food—and the ring is gone?"

"Honest to God, I'll do right by ye."

Jasmine fixed him with a stare and crossed her arms. "Not good enough. We only just met, how am I supposed to trust you with getting food for my children?"

"I'm doing you a favour!" Dougie was all but shouting in his whisper. "I wasne even going to take a cut for my own wains."

Her shoulders sagged and she dipped her head a little, but she said nothing.

"All right," said Dougie, and tugged at his own finger. "I'll give you my ring until you get your food. Call it a safety deposit." Grunts ensued until he finally twisted it loose.

He held it out and Jasmine cupped her palm below. It dropped, glinting gold as it spun in the air. She caught it and held it up, turning it this way and that. "Heavy."

"That's cause it's real, not a trinket like yours! Will ye trust me with it now?"

Jasmine closed her fingers around the gold band and slid the silver one off her finger, gazing one last time at its deep green stone. For a moment she gripped both rings, one in each hand, and a silent sob racked her form. Then she let her ring fall into Dougie's open hand.

"I promise you won't regret this." Dougie raised his hand, hesitated, then rested it briefly on Jasmine's shoulder.

She glared up at him. "I had better not."

"You got it," said Dougie, and backed away before turning to stride into the sunset.

"Drive a hard bargain," she called after him, and spun around, coming face to face with Ellis. "Wait. You were there this whole time?"

"I was," he admitted. "You did right to insist on a bond, so to speak."

"Why?"

"I don't know him very well and you know him less."

"But you do know him." She grabbed Ellis' arm. "Tell me I haven't made a huge mistake."

"Show me his ring."

She handed over the heavy gold and Ellis inspected it. "I'd say this is worth a good deal more than yours. And it really is his wedding ring. He's worn it to work for as long as I can remember."

Jasmine slumped. "Then he really is that generous, that he'd risk me selling this in the meantime."

"Don't break that trust."

"I don't intend to."

Ellis looked down. "Does your husband know you were planning to sell your ring?"

"No. But he'll understand. He has to." She flicked a tear away and gave a tiny smile. "We married right after the Senate took control. It was so hard to find any sort of ring and he somehow got hold of that one. Seven years I wore it…and now it's gone…" She covered her face with her hands and stood, a pillar of sorrow outlined by floating dust motes in the doorway.

Ellis approached with care and placed his arms around her with the lightest of touches. She crumpled, burying her face in his chest. When she calmed a little, he held her at arms' length. "Look at me."

She lifted her face, all red and blotchy, but couldn't meet his gaze.

He gripped her shoulders. "You'll be all right. Now get home to your family. It's you they care about, not a silly old ring."

Jasmine smiled and stepped away. "You're right, of course. Thanks, Ellis."

In a moment she was gone and Ellis remained alone. If he still had Amy, she could sell every blessed thing he owned and he would not mind a bit.

He ambled out through the doorway and blinked at the golden sky of early evening.

The crowd had ebbed fully away, and Jasmine was already well out of sight; yet one figure remained: a familiar figure holding a bicycle.

"Mariah!" He hurried forwards to meet her. "Is everything all right?"

She laughed, and he thought it the sweetest sound in all the earth, especially after the day he'd had. "Yes, Da. Everything's grand. I've got something to show you."

There she stood, so strong, so independent. A miracle in the circumstances. "You're wonderful, you know that? Well, that's what I think."

Mariah pulled a tiny bundle out of her bag and grinned at him sideways. "You old softy. Now look here." She unwrapped the hanky and lifted the last corner—for his eyes only—to reveal one tiny, perfect strawberry. "It's a wild one, Da. I'm going to try germinating the seeds."

The hope in her face made Ellis' breath catch in his throat. Such faith in the future. It was a long shot, but this was his daughter. He hugged her, the fruit safe in her outstretched hand. "If anyone can do it, you can."

FOE OR FORAGER

Liam hung around after work, resting his back on the breezeblock wall and jiggling the sole of his foot up against it. He hoped for a word with Mariah, but she must be staying late again and he didn't want to go back inside or the boss might snag him for a word about the argument today with that silly girl Kitty. She couldn't be more than sixteen, with a good brain in her head, that's why she'd been chosen to work in the Belfast Department of Farming Statistics—keeping the government and the distant World Senate fully informed on the successes and failures of food crops across the North of Ireland. It was really nothing more than data entry, but the selected few were excessively revered by a populace generally regressed to an awe of computers.

Young Kitty preened and prided herself in her position, as well as spending much of the day goofing off with her equally young desk-neighbour Elsbeth. The two of them particularly enjoyed poking fun at Liam and Mariah as the most senior members of the office team. Today, they'd been in fine fettle, shooting verbal barbs and giggling something chronic. If it wasn't an insult to all his imaginable relatives, it was a criticism of Mariah's fashion sense. Admittedly her clothes were more practical than attractive, but nobody deserved that kind of constant harassment. Liam reddened a little. Mariah could wear a sack and he'd still think her the most beautiful thing he'd ever seen.

The latest kerfuffle had arisen when the office manager had left the room for a moment and Kitty had remarked loudly to Elsbeth that Liam's ma and gran must be ugly as sin to produce him. Everyone in the room heard it, there was no getting around that fact, and several laughed in spite of their efforts to resist. He couldn't hold it against them, but as for the instigator…

Liam, at the end of his tether, stood to his feet and faced her. "You little gobshite! You—"

A look of triumph crossed her face as she peered beyond him, so that he buttoned the rest of what he'd been about to say, and turned in time to see the boss frowning in the doorway. He dropped into his seat and Mariah shot him a sympathetic glance.

Surely the boss would not punish him for being driven to madness by that harpy. Still, he wasn't so sure it was a good idea to wait around here longer on the off chance she'd give him a verbal warning. Reluctantly, with a last glance backward in case Mariah should appear, he pedalled off around the corner.

So the first strawberry was gone. Given away in the heat of the moment, in hope of something more. Liam couldn't imagine a better cause…there would be other fruits in good time. He smiled as he thought of Mariah's sweet face, astonished, when he'd placed it in her hand yesterday. Surely she realised now what she meant to him, had an inkling of what he felt for her. After all, the authorities frowned on what they called independent food production. He might even get in trouble for distributing seed. More than once he'd seen his neighbour Peter watching as Liam grubbed in his pathetic bit of backyard. Not that it would ever come to anything.

He'd known Peter since they were wee lads in nursery school, but that was no guarantee of decency. They'd played together, visited each other's homes, and gone exploring in the days when wild blackberries were still to be found in the foothills and around the coastlines. The scoldings had been sound when they'd returned with their clothes stained purple. How deceptively easy it was—to spend countless childhood hours with someone, and yet not know at all what sort of man he'd grown into. But these were perilous times. Folks did what they had to do in order to get that little bit of extra food that might be the difference between life and death for an elderly relative. In a way Liam understood when people gave in to the temptation, but it didn't in the slightest reduce his own danger as he searched for illegal nourishment in the byways of the city. There was no way to be certain that his old acquaintance wasn't a Senate informer out for a reward.

At least Mariah was usually the soul of discretion, not to mention the grandest girl he'd ever met. His heart melted at the thought that she might yet fully respond to him, that she might be his one day. He still had some wooing to do. And woo he would, with all his care and charms, just as soon as he could distract her from her worries about life in general. A difficult proposition in the current circumstances.

It would be hard to find anyone left in this whole country that was still carefree and content. If anyone deserved it, it was Mariah. His heart beat faster as he thought of her, imagined a life together…No. It was too soon for that. He didn't want to ruin his chances by appearing too enthusiastic.

He paused near his secret alley to make sure nobody would see him turn in. The summer evening closed in tight around him, its swiftly fleeting warmth like a traitor's caress. He peered this way and that; the small, mean houses were silent for once, and Liam wondered if everyone had gotten the same idea and all left together before the dimming of the day. It was more than a little disconcerting. He told himself they probably just weren't home from work yet, or they had already arrived and were taking a quiet moment to rest. The breeze softened, gentle with just a touch of evening's chill among the suburban canyons, the muddy expanses of dead yards, the back alleys that ran between the crumbling concrete walls and gappy wooden fences. Above, wispy layers of cloud revealed streaks of jewel blue just beginning to take on a hue of evening glow. These long summer days were at their most impressive when the rain cleared away by sunset; thankfully, this was often the case through May and June. Liam sighed and dragged his eyes back to the ghetto before him.

Was that a scuffle up ahead? The street was still as empty as his stomach, so he entered the alley. On his bike he was tall enough to see over the walls to the forlorn backs of houses to the left and right, where cracked windows protected faded and tattered curtains. Nothing moved except a little water in the ditch from rain earlier in the day. Just once he glimpsed a boy sitting on his back step, tossing a stone into the air and catching it again. The slack-faced child didn't even bother to glance up as Liam passed.

Otherwise the yards were no less deserted than the street. Liam hunkered down over the handlebars and pedalled hard towards the odd little niche with its square patch of viable earth where a tree had once stood within the uneven frame of brick and concrete. He guessed its rotting roots provided much in the way of sustenance for the tiny strawberry plant that had miraculously grown there, and the paving stopped other plants from encroaching and infecting the area with termination genes.

He wheeled around the last bend. In the shadows, a dark figure knelt over the plant, muttering. Liam threw down his bike and tackled the stranger in a single movement, taking him completely by surprise so that a headlock was an easy matter. Near-starvation notwithstanding, Liam's arms were still strong enough to seize the advantage from behind.

"Let me go," the intruder grunted.

"Yeah, right." Wait. Liam knew that voice. "Peter? What the bleedin' heck are you doing here?"

"I could ask you the same thing." Peter shook himself free and the two faced each other.

Liam fisted his hands. He'd prefer not to beat him up, but he would if he had to. "Swear you're not gonna rat on me or by all that is holy I'll lay you low."

"Rat on you—What idjit would do that? I'm just lookin' for food like everyone else. There was a strawberry ripening here the last time I passed."

"Well, eh…"

"You wouldn't happen to know where it went."

Liam wrestled with himself. He'd known Peter forever, and yet…he didn't trust him. Trust was dangerous. He mustered the other man as he shook himself and rubbed at his neck. Glanced in his eyes to look for any sign of dishonesty. He saw nothing, but he knew himself he wasn't always the best judge of people. Suddenly, Liam sighed. Why couldn't he have been born a hundred years earlier, free to choose his own path in life? Sure, there had been Troubles then too, but not like this, of that he was sure. He was tired of standing alone, tired of holding everyone at a distance in case they learned of his mutinous attempts to feed himself and his gran. Surely only the basest of humans would betray another for a basic survival instinct. And he was fairly certain that Peter did not number among the basest.

"You do know." Peter stepped closer, almost into Liam's face. "Scared to tell? Go on wi' ye. I'm about as much a Senate informer as you are a ballerina."

Both burst out laughing. Liam twirled his hand in the air with a flourish, even as he understood that Peter had seen right through him to discern the reason for his hesitation.

Liam looked at his feet. "I gave it to a girl." He flushed a little, but couldn't help smiling as Mariah's face floated in his mind's eye.

Peter clapped him on the shoulder. "Wooo! A girl you like?" At Liam's silent nod, he grinned. "She must be a beaut. Wouldn't mind seeing her myself. Not gonna steal her," he hastened to add.

They laughed again. Liam leaned over to check on the next strawberry—it was still miniscule and greenish-white all over. "That'll be a wee while coming."

"This'll help," said Peter, and uncorked a bottle he'd pulled from his pocket. He poured a quantity of dim liquid onto the earth, releasing a strong smell of ammonia.

Liam screwed up his nose. "Is that what I think it is?"

Peter only nodded. Sure, it made sense. Liam wished he'd thought of it.

"Bit o' that every night and she'll grow stronger."

Liam regarded his lifelong friend and realised once again that he knew him not at all. "How'd you get to be such an expert?"

"You don't remember I went away every summer to me Da's farm…"

"I know you live with your cousins, but I was too small to remember much, you know, from before."

"Me, too. But Da made me learn how to care for the soil, an' I never forgot that. Some things are just in my blood, even though we've got practically nothing to work with now. The principles he showed me still apply. I can hear the memory of his voice, telling me how to treat the greenery with kindness so that it will grow best." Peter looked away. "Then the Troubles came again. They vanished him."

Of course. Anyone who knew anything about farming had been taken to secret research centres to aid in finding a solution to the dead earth and unresponsive seeds. No one knew exactly where they went, since no one had come back in all the seven years of the Senate's regime.

"I guess I'll be off home, then," said Liam, slapping the ripped plastic cover of his bike seat. Unless… "Can I offer ye a ride?"

Peter regarded the rear carrier rack. "That'd be brilliant, actually."

Liam swung into the saddle, and Peter positioned himself on the rack over the wheel, gripping the post, feet wide for balance. "Ready?" asked Liam, and at Peter's curt nod, he kicked off and sent them sailing down the bumpy driveway. At its end, Liam turned left, then soon after that left again, crossing a vast and empty intersection with space for several lanes of traffic. These days, he didn't even need to look and see whether anyone was coming; he simply leaned a little and coasted around the corner without turning his head.

Neither spoke as they passed between rows of houses for a while, homes no doubt once worthy of the tag "quaint", with their plaster or brick and timber fronts. Chimneys of varying sizes jutted from roofs, but no smoke rose from any of them. It was too close to summer even if the residents were able to find rare burnable wood. Lisburn Road, the old A1 highway, was once fully lined with trees at regular intervals; an occasional one still stood, its leaves more occasional still, dragging sustenance from old, undisturbed soil deep below the pavement that walled its trunk. Other trees were cut off near the ground, taken to provide an evening or two of warmth for a family. Bright paint in red and blue still adorned some of the shop fronts that occupied the lower floors of the houses, though they too were residential space of late. Worn painted lines everywhere indicated directions and parking spaces for motorised vehicles, the like of which were hardly seen any more, used only by Senate officials. It was hard to comprehend the sheer volume of cars that would have needed all these delineations and arrows.

The Black Mountain reared up in the canyon left by each crosswise street they passed. Another series of ex-food stores whizzed by, most still bearing an inscription revealing the previous purpose. Pizza. Fruit. Spices. To think that people had been free and able to visit any of these places and buy whatever they wanted. Liam shook his head and sighed.

"I know," said Peter from behind him. "Right rotten shame, what's become of us."

Past St. Thomas's church, looking a little the worse for wear since folk had been pilfering bits of it to repair their leaky dwellings. Liam figured St. Thomas most likely wouldn't mind. After a couple more blocks of houses they reached the corner of the vast City Hospital complex, now mostly abandoned except for those parts turned into

Senate factories and workplaces. Here Liam turned right, away from the hospital, and trundled down a tidy street of brick houses. Another church. And then the Queens University campus.

They passed the main building and Liam momentarily released a hand from his bike's grip to point at it. "Friend of a friend was the last person to graduate from there. An' Naomi was the only one in her class, so she was."

"What's her degree in?" asked Peter.

"Biology." The last department to be shut down by the Senate, only a few years ago, as there'd been hope the students would have made some kind of breakthrough in terms of rejuvenating the soil. But they hadn't. Naomi at least was employed in a fertiliser laboratory, an area she'd studied.

He cut through into the open area between the university and the Ulster Museum, ending up in the Botanical Gardens although nothing really grew there now. Just a few very scraggly trees.

The path spat them out at the embankment, where the River Lagan glistened blue and silver under an equally patchy sky. Liam followed the riverbank north past countless three-storey brick apartment blocks and single-level row houses painted white with doors in faded bright colours. Low brick walls bounded some of the yards, while others had only gaps where hedges had been. Here too were some of the city's most modern houses, built only fifty years before with smooth white walls and flat roofs.

The riverside street came to an end, but beyond the black metal bollards the cycleway continued. They followed the snaking river for almost a mile and a half in total, forgoing the first bridge to cross by the second, close in to downtown. Liam steered them over the River Lagan on the old highway leading almost straight to their destination.

A few more miles brought them to the edge of their suburb of Connswater—past the derelict fast-food joints and the enormous empty shopping mall—and a few more turns to their own street.

Liam braked by his front gate and glanced at the door. His gran would be waiting, and he'd saved some of his lunch for her. "Listen," he said. "I've been trying to forage a bit here and there. To help feed my old gran, she can't work any more. What say we join forces, compare notes?" It was a big ask and he knew it, for he stood to gain more than Peter did. His friend was simply the more knowledgeable.

But Peter grinned broadly. "Sure, an' why not? More fun that way."

"Right y'are."

"Let's meet Saturday after work by Crawfordsburn pub."

"All the way out there?" It was a trip of at least ten miles, and not over flat countryside.

"The old golf course's got loads of potential. I've been meaning to check it out."

Liam blinked. He would have a lot to learn. Now he had a proper ally in his quest to support Gran and impress Mariah. He smiled and offered his hand. "Sorry about the headlock before. I didna know it was you."

"No offense, brother." Peter gripped Liam's hand and shook it. "Here's to good foraging."

"To good foraging."

the fate of the ring

Footsteps trod the cracked pavement between faceless industrial buildings that crumbled to dust and rust more each day. The evening glow was unusually bright, the workers chatting as they wandered home with the prospect of a couple of free hours before going to sleep so they could make it through tomorrow.

Dougie Sullivan harrumphed and clenched his fist tighter around the ring that was probably so cheap it could be defined as a trinket. He was mad at himself for letting the woman have his own real gold ring as a condition of sale; if she traded it away, he'd lose bigtime both financially and in his wife's esteem. That ring was their last-ditch security, enough to buy a few months of full stomachs for the children. He just hoped Jasmine was as honest as she meant to force him to be.

The concrete jungle slowly gave way to more homely areas: small brick houses all in their tidy rows, a century old or more. Occasional pockets of green brightened the terrain where weeds had found the earth nutritious. A group of children kicked a ball around in a short dead-end street, but there was no energy in the game; they, too, would have just finished a long workday and those not old enough to work would be hungry until a parent arrived with a small portion left over from their own lunch.

Dougie knew the route well enough to ignore his feet until they carried him all the way home. He swung around the last corner and slowed slightly, now gripping the ring so hard, it must be imprinting on his palm. Muttered to himself, reciting what he would say.

He stopped on the street, groped for his key and slid it into the door that opened directly from the thoroughfare. "Nora—you home?" Dougie's wife often arrived before him, but it was just as likely to be the other way around.

But now, her footsteps scuffed in the other room before she appeared. "Oh good, you're here. Sheena was hoping you'd kept a bit of your lunch for her."

Dougie's heart broke. He'd been so hungry today, nigh on to fainting, and while he had made himself stop before his ration was gone, the remains were pitiful. Even now the spectre of starvation reared its dire head within him once more, yet his youngest child needed what little he had brought home in the one lidded mug they owned. He hauled it out of his coat pocket and relinquished it while at the same time opening his other hand to reveal Jasmine's ring.

Nora's eyes widened. "Where'd you get that?"

"From my co-worker. To trade. I'll get a ten percent cut—that's standard." He gave a little sigh and showed his vacant finger. "I had to loan her mine as a sort of security."

Nora frowned. "You're too trusting. For that you should get twenty. Think of your own family too."

"Depends on what we get. If it's a good trade…there may be a bonus in it." He didn't want to cheat Jasmine but surely if he haggled hard enough there would be extra.

He stepped away and crossed to the back door of the little house. Outside, he breathed the evening air, scooped up a pebble from the barren yard, and strode to its back wall. A cat screeched its fighting call a short distance away. In a moment, the stone flew over the mews and pinged the neighbour's rear window.

There was hardly time to consider his words before the door opposite flew open and a wild-eyed, lanky teen burst out. "Oh, it's you, Dougie," she said, and relaxed a little. "I thought it were one of them dodgy fellers me Da does business with."

"Actually it's about business," said Dougie. "Where's the place tonight?"

The girl gaped, then darted across until only the two walls and the alley separated them. "You'll have missed them tonight, but tomorrow's at O'Groats. You know it?"

He nodded and thanked her. Too bad it was so deep in Protestant territory. Well, maybe these things mattered less these days though mistrust ran deep. He realised he didn't even know whether Jasmine was Catholic; he supposed that getting her family fed—and his own into the bargain—was ultimately more important. So, too, he would go to O'Groats.

Noon hour. The comparative roar of chatting mill workers filled the dining hall, what used to be a factory shed just like the one they toiled in. Now it was slightly improved by the addition of a collection of ramshackle tables and benches. Dougie slapped down his tray of food a little more forcefully than he ought, but he got lucky. The thin porridge jumped in place and returned to its original position.

Ellis shot him a sideways glance. "Steady on there. Don't want to lose any."

Just a platitude, for it was clear that if a spillage occurred, there would be no shame in prostrating oneself to lick it from the table…or even the floor, if he had the stomach for it. So Dougie merely grunted in response.

But Ellis wasn't done yet. "You've yet to finish that deal, yeah? Well…" Here he leaned in closer. "There's a lot riding on this for the girl. You need to do right by her and not skim extra off the top, ya know."

Dougie silently tipped some of his food into the mug to take home for Sheena. He licked the tray to get every morsel, his face like stone. Of course he knew what was right, but with his wife's insistence on twenty percent, he'd possibly have to land somewhere in between if the takings were decent. Ellis meant well; he had children too, though his son had been dragged off to who-knows-where as a farm hand. There were worse fates, but not many. Dougie thought of his three young ones and a chill ran through him at the thought of a possible separation when they grew tall and strong enough. God forbid. He met a firm gaze from Ellis, whose daughter Mariah was all that remained to him, and swallowed hard. Ellis had stood strong all this time in spite of his losses. And Dougie would put off crossing that bridge unless he was forced to come to it.

Numb hours passed until the knock-off buzzer. When it finally sounded, Dougie shook himself all over to dispel the torpor. Lifted his head and met the eyes of the mother who'd made such a scene yesterday. And who could blame her? She'd lost a son, the same as Ellis. He looked away, impassive. If he let it get to him every time, he'd soon be a wreck.

He turned to go and was almost forced to retreat a step when Jasmine leaned into his personal space. He looked down to avoid her stare, but she poked him in the chest. "Hey. I realised I never told you where I live. It's at Fitzwilliam Square, number nineteen."

"I'll be there with your stuff sometime this evening."

Jasmine squeezed his arm, making him shrink back. "I'll be waiting. And so will the children."

Dougie nodded, but kept it brief. Without another word he stepped away, moved through the hustling crowd, and made for the exit. He passed under the doorway where he'd conferred yesterday with Jasmine, but instead of turning southwest towards home, he pivoted and strode north.

Initially this took him deeper into the industrial area. After twenty minutes of walking, the suburbs took over. But not like his suburb. It might not look much different to an outsider, he mused, except for the odd variations of architectural style which might be for any of a thousand reasons including taste. No, these were the homes of Protestants, and while Dougie wore nothing to identify him otherwise, he was still nervous because they would know he was not local. There had been less violence these many years since most folks had more basic concerns than persecuting a different creed. Of course the hot-blooded youngsters still tossed stones over hotspot Peace Walls after curfew, but it rarely escalated beyond that.

He passed only a few people and studiously avoided eye contact. O'Groats was on a short street almost on the fringe of the dockyards area, but on the wrong side of the tracks. It had been a public house once, in the old days before the Senate shut down the gathering places and sent their employees to manual labour. Folks still wanted to drink, of course, so some of the old haunts hosted occasional black market dealing, turn and turn about. Dougie was not after drink but some of tonight's traders would be—he approached the place with caution, absorbing every movement and sound in case a Senate guard patrol was nearby. Or even the cyborgs. He swallowed a taut laugh. There were only the two cyborgs in all of Belfast as far as he knew, and maybe even in the whole North. The chances of crossing their path was as good as nil. Never happened in all these years and it wasn't about to.

The sign still swung over the door of the ostensibly abandoned pub. Its paint had faded, but the name was still clear enough. Dougie paused once more to listen, then, greeted again by silence, he ducked into the shadowed entrance. The dirty glass door creaked open at his touch and he blinked for a moment in the dimness. There was shuffling, and when his eyes had adjusted, three men faced him, shoulder to shoulder.

Dougie raised both hands, acutely aware of the ring in his pocket. "I'm only here to trade for food."

"Let him past." At the order, the three parted to reveal a drink-lord whose paunch betrayed his illicit gains. Bottles and boxes along with other random debris filled the bartop, which possessed only two undamaged stools. The man sat at the sole remaining table in the room. "What've you got, then?"

Slowly, Dougie reached into his jeans pocket and withdrew the ring. Everyone's hopes rested in it; he clutched it another moment before opening his palm.

The dealer's eyes gleamed and he did not hesitate to grab Jasmine's treasure, his rough fingers scraping Dougie's palm in his hurry. "Where'd you get it?"

"A friend."

"You're new here, we don't know you—isn't that right, boys?" They murmured assent. The dealer tossed the ring and caught it again. "We know what that means."

Toss and catch. Toss and catch. Dougie winced and shook his head.

The tossing ceased. "It means a first-time trade. And that means you get half the going rate and call it a good deal."

Half? Surely nobody could be so heartless. Dougie stuttered before words found him. "But—but mister. Think o' the wee 'uns. I've got three to feed from this trade, never mind the parents."

The dealer eyed the ring close up. "Is that so?" Tell you what. I reckon this is worthless junk anyway, so I'll just give it to my missus. You mind and bring something better next time." He nodded to the thugs and they moved in on Dougie.

But he held his ground. "Mister, I made a promise to that lady that her children wouldn't be hungry tonight. An' she gave me her ring on trust."

"Answer me this, then. Can ye bring something better next time?"

Gulp. "I—I..."

"Out with it, sunshine. Ain't got all day."

"I, uh, might be able to get something in real gold." Dougie's heart sank. It was his greatest secret and last resort to feed his family.

"Well then." The dealer rolled Jasmine's ring between thumb and forefinger. "If you give your word to bring that next time, I'll get you something for this rubbish now."

Dougie gave the tiniest of nods and turned away. He'd have to think hard as to whether he really wanted to do that at all. If he did, it wouldn't be soon—but this crook hadn't set a deadline.

The dealer beckoned one of the henchmen close and whispered in his ear, whereupon the man slipped into a back room. He reappeared holding an armful of supplies, which he laid out before Dougie: two sacks of oats, one of onions, and one of potatoes. Each bag looked to be around two to three pounds in weight. Not a bad haul, though he'd heard of better deals. But one look at the dealer's hard face and he silently bent to the task of stowing the stuff in his knapsack. He considered not saying another word, but he didn't want to burn his bridges so he muttered a quick "Thank you," though it galled him to do so.

"You mind and bring me that gold..." the dealer was saying, but Dougie was already out the door and loping away as fast as he could without looking like he was in a hurry.

As soon as he deemed himself far enough away, he ducked into a doorway to do some repackaging. It would never do to be caught with these sacks, printed as they were with Senate ID. Luckily, he'd brought several cloth bags of his own in case the dealer offered loose goods. His back to the street, he quickly transferred the bags of oats and then the vegetables. He caught a whiff of the onions as he did so—but there weren't even ten, so he probably wouldn't get one in his share. Still, a man could dream. He sniffed appreciatively once more before cinching the top tight and buckling the flap over the drawstring. The incriminating sacks he wadded up and left on the doorstep. They would be someone else's problem to dispose of. The fabric would be useful enough if hidden well.

He crossed the dusking city in haste, but not at a run, for people were still about and would ask questions. A gang big enough would easily relieve him of his load. His mind eased when he exited the

Protestant area, but the industrial zone was empty and eerie this time of night; every little sound set him on edge. Once he thought he saw a group of huddled shadows in a side street and hurried on past, hoping he hadn't been seen. It was getting too dark to see anything clearly. Maybe it was just a stray dog—but one could never be too careful. The looming hulk of the Black Mountain and its neighbours jutted into the skyline above the low roofs of the city. He gazed at the hills, remembering younger days when he and Nora had wandered the heady heights without a care in the world.

Downtown sheltered a little more life. Candles flickered in upper windows here and there, and snatches of muted conversations escaped into the night air. But nobody wandered the streets even though he was sure it couldn't be curfew yet. He had the dilapidated brick streetscape all to himself for block after block, the mountains still peeking through city canyons when the angles lined up.

After an hour or so of walking, he reached Jasmine's relatively inner-city neighbourhood. He found the street easily enough, but not all the houses were numbered—so he counted from the nearest one that was, picked his target and knocked on the door. After a short silence, locks snapped back and a careworn woman peered out.

"Erm—does Jasmine live here?"

"Almost right. Next house over." She tapped the air in front of her face.

He thanked her and made his retreat, feeling her eyes on him all the way. Raised his hand to knock at the next house, but the door opened before he could, and Jasmine herself yanked him inside. "Did anybody see you?"

"Just your one neighbour there." He tilted his head.

"Yes, but which one? There's umpteen of them as live in that house."

"Oh, er. Middle-aged woman. Tall, skinny. Is it important?"

Jasmine huffed. "Aileen. She'll pester us till she finds out we've been trading. Still, could be worse."

"Here's the stuff. Now give me my share and I'll be gone."

She hustled him into the kitchen and measured the oats into her jar, then scooped a tenth back into his bag. The potatoes she counted and gave him one large one. "Hm, there's only six onions. I'll give you an extra potato, how's that?"

Dougie nodded. It was as much as he could expect, even if he hankered for an onion. "I just need my ring, then."

Jasmine delved into a pocket. "Here you go. I'm sorry I didn't trust you at first."

"Fair precaution, I suppose." He grimaced, but it was good to have the band back on its finger.

He had no more words, so he nodded at Jasmine, hefted his much lighter backpack, and departed.

At Aileen's house the curtain twitched—then he heard fast footsteps behind him. He spun, fearing Senate guards or worse.

But it was only Jasmine. She clutched an onion in each hand. "Take these. Our kids don't like them and they won't keep forever." She pressed them into his cupped palms, grinned shyly, and scurried back to her home without another glance.

Tears came unbidden to Dougie's eyes as he packed up and went his way between the ramshackle tenements. It really was, he reflected, only because of the onions.

BUNKER BLUES

Peter Donohue waited by the rusty top gate of the old golf club at Crawfordsburn, absently digging the toe of his shoe into the crumbling dampness of the earth. He spotted a seam coming loose around the edge of the old fake leather footwear and ceased his jiggling—he didn't want to make it any worse, requiring a difficult repair when it fell due. No need to make that sooner by dint of a fidget.

He looked up, stepped away from the wooden gatepost he'd been leaning on, and turned to take in the view of the golf greens falling away below him in gentle layers towards the sea. Of course there was less green than there used to be, but this grass was hardy after decades of sea wind and he thought it had survived a little better than the plants in town. Whether that meant it would also shelter edible greens—that remained to be seen.

The north Antrim coast vanished a little in the haze hanging over the Lough of Belfast, but Peter could still make out exactly where Whitehead ended, the invisible coast beyond it almost parallel to his line of sight. His eyes drifted back to the patches of deeper green in the landscape: once traps for unskilled golfers, now they might be veritable treasure troves of dandelions or who knew what else. He ran through the rest of the list in his mind—weeds of yore now sought for their nutritional value and the simple fact that they still grew while many other plants would not. Dock, plantain, nettle, wild garlic, and maybe even a bilberry bush. Now that would be a real treasure. All these could make the difference between life and death for those who teetered at the edge, not young or strong. Peter's Gran waited at home for any morsel he brought her; some days he failed and only had a portion saved from his work lunch of oat slop—no longer worthy to bear the ancient and noble title of "porridge".

As a child, Peter had spent his summers helping his father at a farm in Antrim, learning the ways of the land and how best to coax a living from it. This was before the last Troubles had come, about seven years ago, and he had grown into a man during the time of greatest tumult and injustice. The farm he'd known as a second home had been requisitioned, its owner also—enslaved for his knowledge of agriculture. Peter had escaped such a fate because he was not there at the time. He wondered yet again what might have happened to his Da, whether he was even still alive. And the small section of garden that had belonged to only him, that he had tended his own self since he was a tiny feller, was it still there? He hoped against hope that it was still fruitful, and that one day he would go back and dig up the stone he'd carved with the words: "For the girl I will marry. P.D." He'd been seven, and particularly taken with the idea after a marriage in the family. Perhaps he'd never marry now, since times were too hard to think of supporting a family, but the stone represented a youngster's golden hope and it would be nice to hold it in his hand again.

A shadow fell across the gravel, accompanied by loud panting. Peter pulled half a grin and looked up at the very red-faced Liam.

"Sorry I'm late. I had this…thing going on."

"Thing? You're going to have to be more specific."

"I was at home, right, about to leave, then I noticed this guy out in the street just watching my house. Waited for ages till he gave up and went away, and what do you know, not thirty seconds after he went off round the corner, there's this ear-splitting sound." Liam touched his fingers to his head.

"Well, what did you hear?" Peter let his tone grow a little exasperated.

Liam gulped. "A motorbike, Pete. A motorbike like only those Senate guards use now."

Peter's eyes widened. "An' he coulda just as easy been watching my house right next to your 'un."

"Aye, that he could." Liam nodded gravely, his red cowlick falling back into his face from where the wind of his travel had swept it up.

"But he ain't here now."

"No, I wasn't followed."

"Then let's get to work." Peter unclenched his jaw and stretched out a hand to indicate the landscape before them.

Liam swung off his bike and walked it through the open gate, leaning it beside Peter's and adjusting the loose branch to cover both. "Oh, yours is working now? That's grand."

"Yeah. I found a junk one with some spokes I could repurpose. This machine should last me a bit longer now."

The bikes hidden as best they could, the two young men strode off to the first tee. Although the day was dry and calm, here they were exposed to the air currents that surely came all the way from Scotland. Peter had once dreamed of going there; perhaps he still would some day.

Twisted, stunted trees lined the fairway, which, although suffering neglect, still bore a decent resemblance to its former self. Peter stopped past the tee area and scanned the green for traps and bunkers that would be of the most use to them now. Darker plants sprouted partway along on the downhill side. He pointed in that direction. "Let's try there."

They loped along on the springy, tough turf. Too bad it was inedible, as it was the only thing truly thriving within sight.

At the edge of the first hollow, Peter grimaced and waded in.

"Okay, so we've got dandelions for sure, but they're so big they'll be hard to digest. And they tend to choke other plants that might make better food."

Liam stooped, rummaged, removed a small leaf. "I've not eaten today. Do ye mind?"

"I'll join you."

For a time they fossicked in the tangle for the baby dandelion greens, the easiest part to chew and indeed the only leaves edible at all without lengthy boiling. They found occasional flowers, which were good eating also, but left most so that the cycle of life could continue. As tough as it was to eat, the dandelion was precious for its toughness in the face of famine. Its next generations must be preserved.

Nothing else grew in that patch, so with slightly fuller bellies they wandered on to the next fairway. Here, bunkers were apparent on both sides. With the merest of nods the two foragers split up and took one each.

Peter stepped down off the solid turf and gaped at an area almost free of dandelions—but rather full of wild garlic. He blinked. Were they in rows? Someone had beaten him to it if so. These were too small for harvest anyway. The earth they rooted in was rich and black; he touched it reverently, wondering how it had been returned to that state, or even stayed that way through all the genetic manipulation and scarcity of humus.

"Nothing here," called Liam. "What about yours?"

Peter leapt back up onto the green and shook his head as he met his companion. That was someone's private garden and he'd not interfere. Still, it gave him hope that they'd find similarly preserved soil elsewhere in this huge area.

They moved on. The next green also had a bunker on each side halfway along; again they took one each. Here was another thicket of large dandelions. Peter carefully turned back the leaves and prodded the ground. It was black, like in the cultivated hollow—no wonder the crops grew so well in it. But some of the dandelions would have to be removed, risking the fragile ecosystem of the fertile patch. Someone must have done exactly that to the fullest possible extent on the last green, which meant the cultivated area was possibly in danger.

Liam came over. "What do you see?"

"Look at this soil. It's alive—it can grow things."

"What about the dandelions? We can't waste them."

Peter had a vague plan for those too. "How about we take some entire plants out, put them in maybe at home or whatever, and try growing something else in between the dandelions that remain?"

"Ooo, that's good." Liam grinned, then his face fell. "But what would we put in here?"

"Something high-yield, I think. Though that will depend on the ground." It was all a guessing game. "Pumpkins are good and plentiful from just one creeper."

Liam salivated audibly. "Where the blinkin' 'eck are you going to get pumpkin seeds that work?"

"I've got a harvest coming on a plant, um, elsewhere." Peter didn't want to give away the hush-hush location of his pride and joy, hidden deep in a patch of forest not far from home.

Liam gaped. "I've not heard of anyone able to grow pumpkins since these Troubles came upon us."

"Well then, it's about time we did, yes?"

They continued on, examining all the bunkers on the course. Some were useless, full of the same inhospitable earth and turf as the green itself. Others held jungles of weeds, and of these a few had potentially good soil. Halfway down they crossed the railway line that curved through the golf course, cutting it in two.

Peter saw no more signs of deliberate cultivation—it must have been a one-off. When they had worked their way down to the black rocks at the shoreline, they sprawled to rest on a patch of spiky grass that grew in the accumulated sand. He poked at it with calloused fingertips. "How does anything even grow in this? So many secrets I wish we could discover, could apply to get other stuff growing."

Liam nodded, his gaze far away on the horizon, then drifting back to the nearby coast where it jutted out. He narrowed his eyes and pointed. "Is that a path just there, or am I seein' things?" It certainly resembled an opening in the trees. "Maybe there's more to this golf course," said Liam.

Peter had never heard of one with more than eighteen holes, but anything was possible—and the forest, if accessible, might be just as interesting to investigate. "Let's take a look, then."

The two linked wrists, as if arm-wrestling, and pulled each other to their feet in one swift motion. The forest path was closer than it seemed and soon they entered the dimness only deepened by the overcast sky. Once his eyes adjusted a little, Peter examined the track and realised it was exceedingly well-trodden for such an isolated location. There was no jungle of inedible undergrowth creeping across the way, no branches poking into its airspace—indeed, on closer inspection, some trees bore wounds old or new where wood had been broken off.

Just in the moment when Peter stretched out a hand to slow Liam's loud and efficient progress through the woods, a voice echoed ahead; truly echoed, as if inside a cave. The two explorers stopped swiftly, silently, and after exchanging surprised glances, proceeded again at a more careful pace. The earthen path swallowed the sound of their footsteps; the voice spoke no more for the moment. Then Liam trod on an especially crunchy leaf.

"Who's there?" The shout from ahead was less echoey this time. A child's voice whimpered and was softly shushed.

Peter shrugged. In for a penny…"Hello?"

As he and Liam advanced another pace or two and stepped around a twist in the track, they almost ran into a big stick held by an old man with a face fierce enough to make Peter almost wish he'd said nothing and just slunk away.

The ancient stood in a square concrete doorway set into the hillside and well overgrown with branches. A musty scent of old stone and damp earth wafted out, along with urine and something else unsavoury that Peter couldn't quite place.

"Get away from here," said the man in a low, steely tone, "and don't you dare ever come back." He shifted his weight to his other foot so that the long club-like rod he gripped in both hands wavered at the tip. "In fact, do yourself a favour and forget you ever saw us."

Liam gulped loudly. "Us? Who's us?"

Two skinny children in ragged dresses appeared at his hip, dirty blonde hair tousled on top. The nearer one grasped the older man's shirt hem, and he exploded at them both. "Back inside. Now!"

The little ones obeyed, but not before Peter met their wide, tear-rimmed eyes. They vanished backwards into the blackness beyond the doorway.

"Uh," said Peter. A belligerent grandfather was the last thing he'd expected back here in the wilds of the untamed coast. Suddenly his breakfast of dandelion salad wasn't sitting so well in his innards. "We, uh, we mean no harm. We were just looking on the golf course for some place we maybe might start a garden."

Grandpa shook the stick. "You leave my patches alone! Or by my word, I'll...I'll—" His words failed him.

"Surely there's enough room for more cultivation up there?" Peter surmised that the tended plot belonged to this family, but it was only one of several potentially fertile areas.

Liam wrinkled his brow. "*More* cultivation?"

The old man relaxed a little, lowered his weapon part way. "I suppose ye're not Senate guards, by the look of ye."

Peter and Liam glanced down at their grey-weathered, threadbare shirts and pants, patched and repaired over and over. "Hmph. You got that right," said Liam.

"Promise me ye'll leave my harvest alone," insisted the man.

Peter didn't have to agree. He and Liam likely had the upper hand in this hard, finders-keepers world. But as he had said, there was enough room. "We won't touch the place you've worked on."

"Wait, where exactly is that?" Liam blinked.

Peter held up a hand to quiet him. "I saw it, pretty close to where we started looking."

"An' ye never said a word." Liam's sidelong gaze sent a chill of guilt down Peter's back.

"It was obvious that it belongs to someone. I wasn't going to mess with it." Peter turned back to the old man. "Listen. Really. We don't intend you any ill will. We'll leave your garden alone, and we'll not tell anyone. We just want a chance to try some of the places you've left alone."

"Ye'll leave me plenty to work with? I have a family to feed." The little girls had snuck up again and peeked around the grandfather's legs.

"Of course. We can't fill the whole area, that would be suspicious and way too easy for others to find."

"Others like you?" the man growled. "They better stay away."

"I meant guards."

Grandpa nodded. "Aye, nobody wants them sniffing around. He swung his staff in his left hand until it met the ground, and extended his right. "Guess we'd better shake on it. It's a paltry hope, but I wish you luck."

Peter wanted to promise help, that he'd share his own harvest, but he had his own Gran to think of and couldn't say yet what the yield might be, though it broke his heart. He extended his hand, gripped the tough and wrinkled one. Then elbowed Liam to do the same.

Formalities completed, they nodded at the old man and turned to go back the way they'd come. They were silent for a long time, but when they emerged from the trees onto the green, Liam poured out his thoughts. "Imagine that, him and the wee-uns living back there in that—that *hole*. And imagine the cheek of him, thinking he can have all this to himself." He swept a hand across the undulations of tees and traps. "Even though he's not using it!" Liam paused for a moment in his rant. "I had no idea people lived like that."

Peter reached over and noogied Liam's scalp. "Anyone ever tell you you're a bit of a hothead to match that hair of yours?"

Liam laughed. "Yeah, all the time. Especially at work, when I have to put up with those young ninnies."

They roved the lower middle section of the open space, checking for any more possible future garden areas and pausing at the dandelion patch to gather a meal for those at home. They crossed back over the railway line and climbed the slopes back up to the top gate where they'd entered.

"How's that girl of yours?" asked Peter, as they freed their bikes from the camouflaging branches.

Liam grimaced. "She's not mine yet, my friend. But I have a feeling she will be, someday soon."

Peter whacked him on the shoulder and both laughed. Then Peter's eye fell upon something that should never, ever be here: a shiny mudguard and its motorbike wheel protruding from an even better hiding place. "Liam," he said, "we've got to get out of here right now."

Liam boggled, and no more was said as they leaped in their saddles and rolled away down the hill towards Crawfordsburn, in whose inn the famous had often sojourned in olden days. Liam chose the main road, no doubt figuring that he'd hear a motorbike coming from a long way off and be able to hide himself in plenty of time if need be.

Peter swung off to the right, towards the coastal route, which was longer, but harder to follow. Even as he rattled down back alleys towards Helen's Bay, his mind's eye was filled instead with visions of green turf vistas all rimmed with food, from the rusty top gate, spanning the railway, and all the way down to the glittering ocean.

He laughed at himself. Now there was a pie-in-the-sky idea.

Mmm, pie.

It sure was nice to dream.

my traitor son

Deborah Naesmith carefully poured water spiked with worm juice onto her pride and joy, the last good apple tree in Bangor. When the ground around its roots was well soaked, she straightened with a groan and rubbed her creaking back with her knuckles. It would be worth it, when harvest time came around again.

She surveyed her little garden, paltry enough as it was, but plenteous for these times. It was only slightly hidden from the road by a row of dried-out hedging, but Senate guards never came up here and her neighbours wouldn't dob in an old lady just trying to feed herself, illegal as it was.

Footsteps sounded next door as Samantha, just less than a decade her junior, returned from work. She waved at Deborah from her front step and cast a glance at the growing greenery. "You'll have to show me how you do that."

Deborah approached the fence and peered at Samantha's yard. "Not looking too bad, now."

"Only because you helped me in the spring. I don't have the time to care for it as I should."

"It would only take a little more effort and you'd soon grow enough for your dinner."

Samantha's eyes glazed over. "All that food…two meals a day! Not that work pays well any more—the lunch is just slop these days."

"All the more reason to work on your garden."

Samantha sighed and nodded. "One of these days, when I'm not so exhausted, I will. You'll tell me all the secrets, right?"

"Aye," said Deborah.

Samantha smiled, waved once more, and vanished inside.

Deborah turned back to her garden, shaking her head ever so slightly. She'd had a similar conversation with Samantha at least once a week for as long as she could remember. Perhaps she was just too scared to try gardening when it had the potential to get her in so much trouble.

She dripped the worm juice concoction along a row of beetroot, ensuring it landed on the soil and not the leaves. As she finished, the front gate squeaked.

"Hullo, Ma!" said Owen.

"Son! It's early ye've come today." All the workers usually finished at six, but Samantha worked in the next bay while Owen's factory was on the far west side of Belfast, so he sometimes didn't get home till seven.

A frown crossed Owen's face, then he grinned. "I improved workflow efficiency today, so they gave me an hour off."

"Workflow efficiency—what's that in English?"

"I noticed the younger kids were talking a lot, you know, fooling around—so I told the foreman and he told the manager. So now there's to be no talking except for work stuff, and today we turned out eight mudguards instead of six."

Deborah closed her eyes. "Child, my child. You're a bond-slave to the Senate. Why would you care if they get eight mudguards a day—and why would you take away what little fun those young ones have in life?"

"Oh." Owen's face fell, but then perked up again. "But Ma. The manager said I might be up for a promotion. You know that means more food."

Deborah regarded the vegetable patch. "We manage, son. We're not starving."

In that moment there came a faint mechanical purr, just enough to tickle her ears. She looked up, towards the city, and Owen did too—so she wasn't imagining it. The sound grew a touch stronger.

"I think that's a motorbike, Ma," said Owen. "I made them there mudguards, so I did." There was pride in his voice.

His mother found herself unable to mirror his broad smile. "Aye, and the only people as use a motorbike is Senate guards, and what good ever comes of that?"

Owen winced slightly. "Sure an' you're right. But wouldn't I love to see one of them in action..."

"You may get your chance if we're very, very unfortunate." Deborah's eyes unfocused as she sharpened her ears. The vehicle grew closer still, so that she thought it would probably go past the end of Cliff Road.

But the moment passed when it ought to have been getting farther away again. Still it increased, and she gripped her son's upper arm. "It be coming down our street. We'd best be out of sight."

"But Ma, can't I hide in the bushes? I might get to see it."

She looked at him sharply, shook her head once, and pulled him, resisting, towards the front door. "You know meeting a Senate guard generally doesn't go well for anybody." It was true—anything could happen from arbitrary punishments to kidnappings and disappearings.

Owen finally let himself be dragged. Once inside, Deborah secured all three door locks. They entered the parlour with all its granny knick-knacks and Deborah passed through the archway to the kitchen, half-turning as she realised she was alone. She looked back into the front room.

Owen knelt in the corner by the window, peeking over the sill.

Deborah gave up. The net curtain would hide him to a degree, and that would only be necessary if the guard looked straight at him, which would only happen if he came right into the garden.

The garden! Deborah withdrew around the wall, a hand to her chest. She hoped beyond hope that her tidy rows of vegetables were hidden enough behind the dead hedge, and that the intruder in their neighbourhood wouldn't take it into his head to look closer.

The invading motor grew louder, louder. Surely it would pass the house any second now, and be on its ill-fated way. She squeezed her eyes shut and tightened fists where she stood.

The roaring engine cut out, leaving silence for her heart to pound in. Owen shot a glance back at her, excitement and fear mingled on his face. The front gate squeaked.

"Ma!" Owen hissed. "He's bringing it in—and what a beauty. Oh, Ma. He's lookin' at the veggies."

Deborah swayed a little, but found the presence of mind to stagger a couple of steps to her favourite armchair. The world still tilted around her. She knew it was coming, but it still made her jump: Four hearty knocks at the door.

"Open up. In the name of the Senate!"

Owen looked to her and she inclined her head towards the hallway. There was no way out but through. "Go on, son."

He shot to the front door and set about unfastening the locks. One—two—three. Hinges creaked. Deborah looked at her knees.

"Owen Naesmith?" The voice was strangely jovial. "May I come in? The Senate has business to discuss with you."

Deborah forced her gaze up. Owen backed into the room, followed by a strutting officer in the dark uniform of the Senate guard. The man gave a stiff little bow towards Deborah. "Er—we do need to discuss this in private."

She opened her mouth, but before she could state firmly that she wasn't going anywhere, Owen answered for both of them. "If my Ma can't hear it, then I'm not interested."

The man pasted on a smile. "If that's how you want it—so be it." He gestured at an empty chair. "May I?"

Owen nodded, and the two men sat.

"You've probably guessed what this is about," said the visitor. "It's come to our attention that you have particular skill in observation, supervision, and situational analysis."

Deborah's racing heart slowed only a little. Owen looked confused for a moment, then grinned. "Oh, you mean today at work? Thanks, I think." He caught Deborah's eyes and she glared at him. His grin vanished.

The officer went on. "Therefore, we would like to offer you a place in the Senate Academy—a three-month live-in course where we'll train you as a guard. After that time you may leave the barracks and return to live here if you wish, though many choose to stay. Either way, you'll be paid well for your work with three large meals a day, and you'll have the best job security in all of Belfast."

"Three meals! Imagine that." Owen's eyes glazed over.

Deborah interrupted his hungry reverie. "What's the actual job description, if ye please?" Of course everyone knew what a Senate guard did, but she wanted to hear it from the horse's mouth.

"Well, ye know yerself, there's patrols, workplace inspections, curfew enforcement, and investigation of illegal activity. And, er, other exciting things."

Like hauling innocent folks from their families, never to be seen again, thought Deborah, but said nothing.

"Oh, and of course you'll have your own motorbike."

"Me own—?" Owen was starstruck.

"And we'll teach you to drive it, naturally."

Deborah could practically see the temptation coiling around her son. Then the final blow fell.

"You should know as well, we show a certain leniency to the families of Senate guards and trainees. You're completely free to decide what you want to do, but if I don't see you at training on the morrow,

I'll be forced to report your little growing operation here." He flicked his gaze towards the front window. "That could have different outcomes depending on what the higher-ups decide, but I can tell you good gardeners are always needed up at the Antrim farm camps. No matter what age."

Yeah, 'cause you keep killin' 'em via starvation diet. Horror flooded through Deborah. She managed to keep from trembling, but as Owen looked to her she knew he couldn't miss the fear. His expression hardened. *Oh my Lord, he's going to do it.*

"So I have until tomorrow to decide?" said Owen to the officer.

"Aye. Be there at eight sharp if you're coming. No need to pack, we provide everything." The man handed Owen a card with an address on it. He stood. "I'll be off then, seems like you two have some things to talk about."

He reached the front door in two long strides and let himself out, shutting it quietly behind him. There were soft footsteps in the gravel, then finally the roar in the street as he brought his machine to life.

Owen stood openly at the window now, watching as the visitor rode away. He remained there, staring out, for long seconds after the sound had abated to a tiny buzz and then to nothing. Deborah only realised she, too, had frozen in place, when his solid silhouette finally shifted against the light, his shape a burned outline on her retinas. She blinked the ghost image away and shuddered a little at the resolve on her son's face. "Don't do it, boy o' mine. It's not worth it. It be like selling your soul for three square meals."

"Aye, Ma, I see that, so I do—but what about you? If I don't go, they'll take you away."

Life as they knew it would be over either way. "Dinna worry about me, lad. I'll go into hiding. I know some folks at the squatter camp out past Groomsport. They'll surely take me in until this blows over."

He ran his fingers into his dark curls and gripped them hard. "That camp's the first place they'll look. And d'ya think they'll ever stop watching this house for ye to come back?"

Into the momentary silence, her stomach rumbled. They both grinned, though it was an effort. She wobbled to her feet and pointed to the kitchen. "Get the stove going, will you, while I pull a couple of those beetroot for our dinner?"

Owen made a face—beetroot wasn't his favourite—but headed for the back door and the woodpile.

Half an hour later, they sat at the kitchen table over a mess of red and green: the beetroot, and its stalks, and its buttery leaves. Good food all of it. Owen swallowed, his gaze far away, and Deborah wondered if he was thinking about the barracks food he'd been offered. No doubt it would be more varied—and more to his taste—than what he got here at home. And yet, if he didn't go, her little garden would be a casualty.

He took a gulp of water from the wineglass, their last remaining. "Ma, you can't hide from them. You'd end up on a farm for sure, and then how long would you last?"

"Even if it happens that way…" Deborah reached out and laid her hand over his. "I'll be glad you didn't have to do those evil things."

Owen forked another cube of beetroot and peered at it as one might examine a snail. "And I'd feel nothing but guilt the rest of my life, that I let you suffer so I could get out of it."

He chewed and forced the mouthful down, then brightened. "Think, Ma. If they give me as much food as he said, I'm sure I can bring some of it home to you."

"Child. It's not worth it."

They fell together into a deep silence, in which they moved around each other as they cleaned up and prepared for night. The evenings were long this time of year and often they'd sit by the back door and watch the sea between the houses in front. But neither was in the mood tonight. When Owen fled to his room before it was even fully dark, Deborah discovered that she, too, was extraordinarily tired and went to lie down, although she was certain she couldn't sleep.

The next thing she knew, morning light filtered in through her grandmother's drapes. Something had woken her—but what? As her still-drowsy mind struggled to awaken, an unnamed dread weighed her body down.

Then yesterday's events slammed full force into her awareness, and she shot upright. Her bare feet landed on the floor, and she shrugged a rumpled housecoat over her nightdress.

The front door shut.

"Owen!" she called, yanking on her bedroom door. His room stood open and unoccupied across the landing.

She almost tumbled down the stairs in her haste. The house was quiet. Too quiet for this early in the morning. Surely he wouldn't just leave—not without saying goodbye? Perhaps he was afraid she'd try and talk him out of it, which they surely both knew she would. Or maybe he was more afraid that she'd succeed.

In a daze she stepped into the parlour, so musty and empty of life with her son's sudden absence. Her gaze passed unseeing over the oft-patched armchairs, the cushions she'd sewed and embroidered in older times when such leisure was a legitimate pursuit. She padded into the kitchen, more out of habit than anything else, and immediately spied the folded page propped against the kettle. A sad smile crossed her face. Her boy knew exactly where she could be counted on to find it without delay.

The stove's embers still glowed; he must have set it going. She stoked it absently and placed the already-filled kettle on its cast-iron top before settling on a chair and unfolding the letter.

Dear Ma,

I'm sorry to take off like this, but I can't let you stop me. Your life will be in danger if I don't go. I couldn't live with myself if they took you away. I wish there was another solution. At least this way, we won't be parted for long. I'll visit whenever I can during training and come back to live at home after, if you'll have me.

I am giving up less than you would lose. Maybe I can quit once they forget about your garden.

Love you, Ma. Never forget that.

Owen.

Deborah read the words over and over again, through a building haze of tears. The tightness in her throat threatened to strangle until at last she laid the paper down, her head sank onto her hands, and she wailed for her child's lost innocence.

When the flood lessened, she straightened, wiped her face, and carefully fed the page into the flames. Talk of quitting the Senate Guard was a dangerous thing. When the fire had done its job and only ash remained, the kettle began its whistle.

She shook herself and reached for the tea caddy. It was a rare treat she usually saved for special occasions, but she absolutely needed it now.

When it was drunk and the used teaspoon of leaves set to steep for a second cup, she lifted her head and bethought the garden. There was still work needing done, no matter that her world had fallen down. Weeds to pull—some of them edible, which she'd have for her lunch—seedlings to check and irrigate, precious seeds to plant, saved from the small courgette for which she'd traded several of her apples in a back alley.

She gripped her trowel and the saucer of seeds, and stepped out into the front garden. Surveying her small domain, she felt a flicker of pride, but it vanished in a flash: this garden was not worth what Owen was paying for it—right now, and for the duration of an indefinite future. Sure, he wanted to quit later, but if he did, they'd have to move somewhere else. The Senate authorities wouldn't just forget her, certainly by now her skill as a gardener was noted in the records and would be mentioned any time they needed to put pressure on her or the boy. She knelt, dug in an empty patch, fingered the ailing loam.

Now, where was that stack of seedling punnets? Oh, she'd left them inside. She re-entered the dim hallway, and located the tubs as soon as her eyes adjusted. With them in hand, she turned and stood blinking on the doorstep for a moment.

"Deborah!"

She dropped the containers and they rolled away. Damn. Couldn't afford to break any—there were no more to be had. She cracked open her eyes in the glare that penetrated the clouds.

It was Samantha, over the fence. "Are ye all right?" She appeared not to notice Deborah's wooden nod, for she went on. "Listen, I forgot to tell ye last night. There's a…meeting tonight you should probably be at."

"Meeting?"

"Yeah, me colleague told me yesterday. For folks as want to grow more food." Samantha indicated Deborah's garden. "An' just between us, ye're quite good at that."

Deborah swiped at her suddenly-damp forehead. "More food?"

"Aye. They're meeting in the old Bangor foodcourt, tonight after work hours."

"Tonight," said Deborah, faintly, and sat down hard on her front step. *I don't want anyone to know about my…my traitor son.* It was useless. They'd find out. She'd have to tell them. But that was a problem for another day. Of course she was foolish to think the neighbours wouldn't notice when Owen came back on a motorbike. Foolish to write off Samantha as just a dumb and ditzy blonde.

"You okay there?" repeated Samantha. "I have to go to work now."

"Thankye, Samantha. I do believe I'll go to that meeting."

When her neighbour was gone, Deborah gathered her plant pots, eased herself onto the dirt, and seized the trowel; there among her own dangerous greenery, she worked, and fresh tears fell freely onto the earth.

WEB OF TYRANNY

Andi Sumner trod cautiously towards police headquarters, careful to time her morning arrival just so. It had to be after the cyborgs had returned from their night patrol and vanished to plug themselves in or whatever it was they did during the day. It also had to be before she could be considered late, risking a penalty such as a pay cut or overtime. She did not want to see the two cyborgs stationed here—they were terrifying, with their metal limbs and hidden bullets, but even worse than their defacement was the awful look in the eyes of the male one. The female, thankfully, wore shades at all times, though she'd heard it was because some of the wiring went straight into her eye.

Andi shuddered and steadied herself, then swung around the corner of the building to a clear street. Whew. She sagged a little with morning sleepiness as she dragged herself up the five steps to the entrance.

Andi worked for the Senate Guard. This was not a truth she liked to acknowledge, but she reasoned to herself that these days, everyone worked for the Senate in one way or another. It was the Senate that allocated jobs, that provided her so-called "pay" of a dollop of porridge each noontime. She'd worked here seven years, since she was just twelve—practically ever since the Senate took over. It didn't take long until they pulled all the kids out of school and set them to work. Like her friends, she'd thought it a grand lark until they'd sent her here and told her to keep the building spotless or starve—and if she ran away, they said, they'd send her parents to workcamps. She hadn't known what that was at first. She knew now. After several years as cleaner they'd brought in another kid and upgraded her to administration. Day by day she processed personnel files for the guards, who volunteered, who was forced and how—often via threats to the family.

In the hallway she passed two officers, who glanced at her and resumed their hushed gossip. Andi heard every word as if they'd meant her to.

"Chief's wife went and left him."

"So that's why he's in such a black mood."

Gulp. Andi must stay out of his way at all costs today.

She slid into her tiny cubby of an office with "File Room" painted in neat letters on the door. Once settled on the wooden stool, she reached for the first file in her in tray. A new guard for training—and not a transfer from elsewhere either—the poor sod. "Owen Naesmith," she murmured, and opened the heavy record book to the "N" page. There she entered all his details, including that his mother had been threatened with workcamp. Her gaze flitted down the form and her pen hovered a moment. It would be better for Owen and his ma if she neglected to add this part about the ma being a good gardener, but then Andi would get in serious trouble if anyone ever compared the record book to the original form which would be stored in the filing cabinet. Well…there was just a small space left on this line in the logbook. No need to start a new line and waste resources. She grinned. Her boss had told her that often enough. In the tiny space she lettered one word: "Gardener", but ever so slightly messily and small enough that it might just escape notice.

She filed Owen's form away and grabbed for another. Before she could start reading it, the door opened and her boss entered. She couldn't think of him as a police chief, although technically he was; his stout figure indicated his high position, and frankly, he came in here far too often for her liking and stole too many chances to pat her shoulder or elsewhere in passing. She pasted on a frown, hoping it would make her look ugly.

The boss shut the door behind him. *Uh-oh.* He took up the entire floorspace in front of her small desk; she was very glad it stood between them.

He plunked down his fists and leaned over it. "I noticed you were a minute late just now," he said. His tone was amiable, but his beady eyes glittered.

"Sorry, sir. Won't happen again, sir." It wasn't true, but there was no point arguing the matter with him.

He leaned closer so she could easily see his wrinkles and the individual strands of receding salt-and-pepper hair. "All right. Just give me a wee kiss quick-like and we'll say no more of it."

She slid back against the filing cabinet, gaping, unable to speak. As it turned out, she didn't have to.

The boss straightened and a terrible coldness came into his eyes. "Am I that disgusting to ye, then? Well, we'll see about that, so we shall."

In a moment he was gone with a bang of the door, leaving her trembling and perspiring, but mercifully untouched...for now at least.

Andi worked the rest of the morning with a sort of unnamed dread hanging over her. She dragged herself to the canteen for lunch, ate her assigned slop while ignoring flirty guards, and not for the first time she bemoaned her pretty face. Why couldn't she have been born ugly, so they'd just leave her alone? Not many people were truly ugly though, she reflected. Perhaps it was just the general lack of women around here. Oh, there were a couple of ladies that did cooking, and the cleaning girl, but she was largely alone in the building with all these hot-blooded young fellows. Like as not she'd have her peace if she hooked up with one of them—then she'd be his, and the others wouldn't interfere. But she had no interest in such political liaisons.

After eating, she slunk back to her office, head down, deliberately unaware of the appreciative gazes that would certainly be directed her way. Ah, well. Perils of the job, she supposed.

Not long after, her door crashed open, the boss standing in the doorway with an odd look on his face. "The farm draft officer is here," he said. "He's just checking the map for a street to collect able-bodied workers from."

"Um, okay." Andi knew the draft officer by sight, he wasn't a bad sort except for the part where he forced people to leave their homes and never come back, for the most part. Her boss didn't shift or explain a reason for his announcement. "You haven't changed your mind, then?" He tapped his cheek.

She flushed bright red. "I, uh…" In all truth, she'd pushed him from her mind in the hope he'd forget his juvenile desire. No such luck.

When she remained speechless, he grunted. "That's that, then." And he left.

What was all that about? Mind abuzz, Andi attempted to return her attention to the file on her desk. Minutes later, there was a single knock and the draft officer entered. *You'd think this was a railway station,* thought Andi, but said nothing.

"Andi Sumner?" the man said, a tinge of disbelief in his voice.

She nodded, frowning while he peered at her as if this were a goods inspection.

"Stand up," he said. She barely came up to his shoulder. "Turn around." He twirled a finger. "Hmm." He pressed his lips together and vanished, slamming the door.

Moments after that she heard her boss shouting, though she couldn't make out the words.

Was he yelling at the officer? It was hard to feel sympathy for an individual whose job was basically to kidnap people.

Her door burst open again, this time without a knock, and the draft officer stood before her once more. The boss hovered some distance behind, and the officer shot him a sour look before speaking.

"Andi Sumner, you have been selected as a farm worker, effective immediately. You will remain here today while I draft a few more, and the group will leave here when I return with them." He looked bored, rattling off a speech he no doubt knew backwards and forwards from repeating it to everyone he took.

A great buzzing filled Andi's head, and his words filtered through it as if from far, far away.

His monotone continued. "If you vanish between now and then, we will take your parents instead. If you comply, we will inform them of your change in assignment." All this said, he turned and stepped away, leaving the boss gloating a few steps beyond.

Andi looked up at him in a haze. "You did this. You made him pick me."

There was no need to ask why. She'd balked at kissing him, and theoretically had therefore also refused anything that might come after.

The cold, hard look in his eye now said he no longer wanted her like that; but he did want her to suffer. "Them's the breaks, kiddo, when you don't obey your betters," he said. "You mind and do what they tell you on that farm, hear me?" Then he, too, departed.

The door swung open; Andi forced herself to her feet, closed it firmly, and leaned against the inside, shaking. So all of this was over. She'd have a few more hours of privacy here in her own office before she'd have to leave it forever. Suddenly its dingy walls were a comfort—surely more like home than the place she was headed.

The awful reality of it swept over her and she sank down against the door, letting the silent sobs come. To think that today's cheery goodbye to Ma and Da was the final one; to think that she'd slept the last time in her own bed with her orange cat Hunter curled on her feet. She had nothing with her, of course—no change of clothes, not even a toothbrush, but she supposed darkly that she wouldn't need it, seeing as she was only to be a worker drone.

She looked at her spindly arms and despaired. No wonder the draft officer hadn't wanted her—but he had to do what the boss told him.

The hours passed in a daze. Andi managed to process a couple more personnel files, though she couldn't vouch for the correctness of the details she entered in the logbook. As the end of the day approached, she composed herself, wiped her eyes on her sleeves, and waited.

Finally, there was a knock at the door. When it didn't burst open for once, she breathed deeply, stood, stretched, and reached for the handle.

It was her boss. "They're waiting for you outside," he said, and stood aside a little.

Unsuspecting, she made as if to pass him. Then his hands were around her head and he was mashing his face into hers, a lick here, a nibble there. She struggled and squawked until he covered her mouth with his and forced his tongue between her teeth.

Eww. She bit down. Hard.

He let out a strangled cry and withdrew, reaching for his tongue with both hands. It might have been a funny picture in other circumstances, said the small piece of Andi's mind that remained calm.

"You're—you're a monster!" she spat, and dashed away towards the exit and her fate.

She scrubbed at her face, but couldn't wipe away the hot, red shame that covered it. Her eyes stung. So much for composure.

She stepped outside and found the draft officer and a clutch of boys about her own age.

"Since when are ye drafting little girls?" said one of them, bitterly. "'T'ain't right."

"Shut it, we'll have no insubordination," said the officer. He might have said more, but there was the sound of a motor and a van chugged around the corner, another guard at the wheel. He pulled to a stop, but left the engine idling as he leapt out to open the double back doors.

The draft officer nodded at the yawning mouth. "Right then. Get in, all of ye."

The boys grumbled, but shuffled to climb aboard. Andi found herself last; there were no seats, and the others had arrayed themselves on the floor, leaning against every available part of the walls. Cautiously she crawled onto a small floorspace and hugged her knees in front of her, feeling all the eyes facing her way.

Then there was a hand on her shoulder. She recoiled.

A tickle of breath in her ear. "Good luck." It was the draft officer.

The doors slammed and locked, and all light vanished but for a very little that came in through the cracks. The suspension jiggled a little as the driver got in, and the front door shut.

Andi wasn't prepared for the lurch as the vehicle took off; neither, apparently, was the young lout immediately in front of her. She found herself sprawling squashed against the back doors with him on top— doing *what?* "Get your hands off me!" she yelped, striking at him in the dark. He laughed flatly, and squeezed.

She screamed, ending in a broken sob.

Another voice cut in. "Leave her alone, ya maggot. She don't deserve to be here any more'n we do." It was the fellow who'd earlier made the remark about little girls. There was an unseen chorus of mumbled agreement.

The "maggot" pulled away, if a little slowly, and Andi leaned against the doors, hugged her knees even tighter this time, and cried silently, hoping the motor would drown out the sound of her ragged breaths.

The drive went on interminably—a rattling, rackety hell. Andi's head hurt, from nausea, from grief, and from thumping it on the door's locking mechanism behind her when they hit each bump in the road.

When movement stopped, she was almost too dazed to notice. The suspension bounced again and there was the creak of large hinges. They moved forward a little, stopped again, the gate clanged shut, and the vehicle moved on once more.

By now all the stopping and starting had roused her to a state of awareness, more or less, by the time the engine cut out. There was movement outside, and just in time she scrambled away from the doors so she wouldn't fall out.

When they opened behind her, she recoiled from the lecherous face of the lout, and, turning, she blinked at the harsh daylight.

"C'mon, haven't got all day," said someone outside, and contenting herself with the evillest look she could muster for the maggot, she turned her back on him and wobbled out to stand on the hard-packed dirt. She looked up slowly and took in the wide yard entirely consisting of the same dirt, and some simple wooden huts lined up nearby.

Beyond were tall fences that blocked all sight; only the distant hills loomed above in places. Her eyes widened—were those trees on the hills? More than had been seen in town for many years, that's for sure.

"They sent me this tiny woman?" said the same voice as before. "She must have done summat really bad."

"Slut," said the maggot loudly.

"Shut it," said another boy.

Andi was too empty to protest the insults; she looked up at the guard, a farm supervisor, no doubt. He looked her up and down, quite greedily she thought.

He spoke. "I'm Encian Jack,, I'll be your foreman here on the farm. There's not much to it—just eat, sleep and work. All your cares are taken away."

He waved them to follow. They trudged past a few of the bunkhouses until Encian Jack chose one. "Here it is," he said. "Eat your dinner and go to sleep. You'll be glad of the rest." To Andi he said, "Sorry, luv, we don't have girls' dorms."

The boys in her group hurried to join the huddle of weary workers around a large tureen in front of the shack. Andi followed, still in shock, then found a bowl pushed into her hand by the boy who'd spoken up for her. She managed a weak smile as thanks. Dinner...such a nice concept. Never a certainty at home. She ate the serve of porridge mindlessly, then groped her way into the hut, found an unoccupied bunk, and collapsed.

Andi applied her hoe for the first time with vigour. A long sleep followed by a decent breakfast—porridge again of course—had lightened her spirits somewhat, and nobody had molested her in the night. She smiled grimly. It was a poor life when that was a major achievement.

She wrinkled her nose. Sure was stinky, this manure they had to hoe into the field. The brown expanse spread endless before her, unless she raised her eyes to the far-off fences and the glimpse of emaciated forest beyond. Workers dotted the field, each equipped with a bucket and hoe.

As minutes wore on into hours, her newfound strength vanished. By the time a lunch tureen was brought to the field gate, she could hardly drag herself towards it. Muscles ached and twanged that she never knew she had. At least there was lunch to look forward to.

But when she got to the pot, it was bare, and no supervisor in sight. She almost wept, but decided she'd done enough of that lately, and dragged herself back to her hoeing. She worked slower, to spare herself a little; Encian Jack came by and yelled at her.

At knock-off time she gathered herself and prepared to sprint to dinner, so she wouldn't miss it. But her shoe caught in a dip near the gate of the field, and she fell headlong, face first into the smelly muck. She managed to turn her head and spit out the foulness in her mouth, but there was nothing else left. Nothing. She lay there and closed her eyes.

A shadow fell over her. "Just let me die," she moaned.

"Here, you two, you carry her back to the lodgings," ordered Encian Jack. She was lifted and her arms placed across strong backs, and opened her eyes just enough to ascertain that neither of her helpers was the tormentor from the van. She let them take her, feet dragging, out of the field and along the muddy track.

"No, not there." Jack again. "Take her to the supervisors'

barracks—we'll have to find something else for her to do. Say, wash that mud off her first, will you?"

Andi's heart sank. She couldn't face the possibilities in her state of mental and physical exhaustion: what did they consider a wash in this camp, and what would she have to do? There was a squeak and the sound of running water nearby. Her supporters let go, leaving her teetering, then a second later the cold water hit her from above. She gasped and returned to full consciousness as juvenile snickering emanated from a cluster of the men watching, and took in the bucket being filled for another go, as well as the brownish rivulets that dripped from her clothes.

Twice more they doused her, until Encian Jack deemed her clean enough on all sides. "You lot quit staring and get along now," he commanded, then to Andi, "Come with me."

Beyond the regular shacks sat the staff hut, its build only slightly better than the rest. But once she stepped over the threshold, Andi saw that it was much more comfortable—no upper bunks, and some residents had even hung curtains between the beds to create semi-private alcoves. It was to one of these he led her, while snapping his fingers at a guard by the steaming cookpot.

Andi sat on the edge of the bed and received the boiled potatoes gratefully. When she had eaten a few bites, the warmth sliding down her throat like a little piece of paradise, she dared look over to where Jack was taking his own meal. "What's to become of me?" she asked, surprised by the frailty of her own voice.

"Horizontal labour, luv, soon as I'm done here."

No… It was all Andi could do to maintain her grip on the bowl.

The other guard leapt to his feet. "Encian! Ye can't be serious!"

"Dead serious, Jim." His glance ran down her again.

"Look, man, would you really want to make her life a living hell, more than it is already?"

Andi stared at the speaker, Jim, and wondered why he wanted to be her advocate.

"What about us, then?" was Encian's retort. "Aren't we in hell too—and aren't we entitled to take a little pleasure when it falls into our laps?"

"Yeah, aren't we?" Another man spoke up from the corner, hungry eyes drilling into Andi.

"No, we're not, not when it would harm another." The other man advanced a step on Encian, who continued to eat.

Andi watched, horrified, her potatoes forgotten. Their voices had been increasing in volume; now they shouted.

"She's not fit for physical work, so she might as well serve staff morale."

"Morale? You're one to talk."

"Aye, and you'll get your turn too, boyo, never fear."

The door burst open and more guards piled in. "What's all this ruckus?" said one.

"Encian thinks that girl should be our whore."

"That tiny thing? How'd she end up here?"

"I've a daughter her age. I'll not let you do that."

"Yeah, what if that was my sister, what then?"

The man in the corner stood up. "She isn't anyone's sister."

Encian nodded at him. "See, at least two of us agree. And I'm the foreman. It goes on my say-so."

Jim leaned into Encian's face. "You just call yourself that. All you do is the paperwork—you're not really the boss, you know."

Encian growled. He surveyed Andi's cowering form again. "Aye, well, are ye seriously suggesting she can be a supervisor?"

There was a chorus of agreement, and a few grumbles too. The majority, however, was clear.

He turned to Andi. "You'd better make them slackers work, or it's back to the original option."

Andi set down her bowl. Her stomach roiled. Safe, for now, thanks to this surprisingly decent collection of Senate men.

Soon the lights went out and hushed conversations died out one by one. Andi lay awake for a long time, intensely aware of the slightest sounds. She couldn't trust Encian to keep his word.

But perhaps she could trust the others to protect her.

SCUM OF THE EARTH

The muted sounds of morning filtered slowly into Darian's waking consciousness. Sleep-dazed colleagues shuffled about, murmuring snatches of low conversation. Darian stretched, pressing against the walls at the head and toe of his end-position bunk—noting with pleasure that nothing hurt today. Six years of hard labour certainly built a man's muscles—even if the barely adequate nutrition meant he didn't carry even an ounce of fat.

He swung upright and wrinkled his nose. The bucket bath last night hadn't been particularly effective against the stink of the manure he'd dug all day yesterday. But that was too bad, since he wouldn't get another turn with the bucket for days. He lurched to his feet and joined the crowd around the water bowl by the door, cupping a little to wet his throat and a little more to rub on his face.

The porridge tureen had already arrived outside. Darian snagged a bowl and dipped it full, taking care to lick all the drippings off its outside as a priority.

"Greedy bugger," said the next in line as he dipped his own in exactly like manner.

Darian shrugged. First in, first served, that was the way it went. He crouched, leaning on the wall of the shack, and slurped the miserable food, watching as the last few sleepyheads tottered out towards the pot.

Regular food was supposedly the great drawcard of the farm camps, at least according to the propaganda. For sure, three bowls a day was more than anyone got in the city—except the guards, of course. Workers regular got just the one bowl at noon for their pay, but they got to live in their own homes with their own people and go foraging for their suppers. Those were workers like his Da and sister, but no, he mustn't let himself think, it'd only hurt. Not yet. It was too early.

No chance of family or forage here, but no need, either: the tureen was always filled and ready when they returned from the field.

Darian wiped the inside of his bowl with a finger and inspected it to make sure he hadn't missed the tiniest morsel. Already the meal was hitting the spot, and he stood, energised for the day. When all his colleagues were ready, the guards moved them out and they joined their work teams in the space between the two rows of huts. He nodded to a couple of his field mates, then set off at a steady stride right behind Encian Jack, the camp foreman and manager of his particular field—not to mention the meanest guard on the farm. Darian had discovered he could escape some arbitrary penalties by simply being the first onto the field each morning.

He peered at the sky; it was practically all there was to look at, here between the tall fences. The day was overcast but he'd put his money on rain later, if he had any money, that is.

Encian Jack reached their field entrance and stopped there to ensure the whole group entered. Darian kept his face carefully blank. Jack sneered at him as he passed by him in the gate, but could not fault his fervour.

Darian quickly filled a bucket with manure from the vat by the gate, grabbed a hoe, and immediately made for a far back section of the field. That was another advantage of being first: Jack rarely visited the farthest reaches, and the less one saw of him, the better.

Also, with any luck, no one would see his tears.

The memories pressed in on him now, as they did every day without fail. He had learned to let them come when he was alone in the field—it was better than sobbing in the bunkhouse where everyone would hear him. Even though he heard the others when they wept in the night.

Thick and fast the images came now, and he gave himself over to them.

It had been a year or so since the Senate took over, abolishing cash and private enterprise and transferring the workforce to bonded labour. Soon enough, his Da had been assigned to a grain mill; his sister Mariah to office work. But no instructions came for Darian. Since he did not work, he could not be paid in meals—his family members saved some of theirs as they could, and he foraged with other jobless young men from his area. He and his friends did think it was strange they'd been left alone.

"Mark my words," his Da had said, "they've got plans for all you strong young blokes." How rightly he'd seen it.

That night he'd come in hungry, having found only a miserable handful of edible weeds. His dog had dug up a nest of field mice, and though she dropped one at his feet and nosed it towards him, he wasn't able to bring himself to eat it. Perhaps that day was coming, he thought, but it was not yet here.

Mariah interrupted his musings, bursting into the kitchen with more energy than anyone should have. She slumped into a chair, slid her container of leftover porridge at him, and took Jemima's head in both her hands to greet her. The dog responded with a lick to her nose, and Mariah buried her face in the long, silky fur. "How was your day?"

Darian pouted at her between slurps. "No good. Hardly found anything at all." He drained the cold sludge and cleaned out the dregs with a finger.

"You poor thing. I can't imagine why they haven't got you working. Wasn't Da going to ask his boss if you could go along to the grain mill with him?"

Shrug. "I'm not sure I'd be any better off."

Mariah glared at the empty container. "I would be." She patted Jemima's head once more and stood to her feet. "Da should be home any minute, maybe he's found something out."

Then, sudden sounds from the street. A brief screech of brakes, running feet, muffled shouting. Darian and Mariah locked gazes for a moment, then, carefully, without making a sound, they edged towards the front window and peered out.

A large white van stood parked at the corner, and a clutch of Senate guards milled around in front of the first house. A woman stood on the step, her face in her hands.

"Say, that's Joe's ma," Darian whispered. As they watched, Joe himself emerged, looking none too happy. He laid a hand on his mother's shoulder; she grabbed him in a hug, and when she showed no signs of letting go, the guards tugged her son away. Joe let them escort him to where he climbed into the van and disappeared. A few of the guards remained there, while the rest moved on to the next house but one. "Samuel's," muttered Darian, then turned wide-eyed to his sister. "They're coming for all of us fellas. Just like Da said."

Mariah seized his arm. "You can hide. Quick, get up in the attic. They won't think to look there."

"I'd much rather get out of the house and completely away." He rushed for the back door, taking only a moment to peek out the narrow window beside it—but a moment was enough to see several guards posted in the mews. "Right. The attic."

He bounded up the stairs, unhooked the attic hatch, and let down its rickety ladder. Mariah stood at the foot to steady it, Jemima whining at her knee. Darian shimmied up, then peered out before pulling up the ladder and preparing to close the hatch. "You'd better go downstairs. You'll have to talk to them, you know."

Mariah gulped. The poor thing, only seventeen, but she was his only chance. "You can do it." He caught her faint grin as he hauled the hatch shut.

"C'mon, Jemima," came her voice from below. There was one more whine, then the patter of claws fading down the stairs.

Darian surveyed the small area. Dim light filtered in between roof tiles. There was a bit of old junk and boxes lying around, but the best place to hide was undoubtedly behind the chimney. Slowly he made his way across the ceiling struts and wedged his lanky frame into the small, triangular space.

Just in time, too—there came a pounding from the front door that shook the whole house. Some shouting, the click of locks, and the soft tones of Mariah's voice although he couldn't make out what she said. He strained his ears, but it was no use. Screwed up his face, sudden remorse stabbing his conscience. Leaving his little sister to deal with Senate recruiters all by herself? He laid his forehead on his knees and hugged them tighter.

Booted feet in the downstairs hallway. More shouting. Then they were on the stairs. He listened as they tromped through both tiny bedrooms, shoving furniture aside, rifling through closets—not that they held much.

Mariah's voice, louder. She must have followed them upstairs. "I told ye, he's not here."

"Then where is he?"

Into the silence that followed there came a single whine. *No, Jemima…* Darian froze.

"Here, why's the mutt looking at the ceiling?"

"There's a hatch!"

"Get it open."

Under concerted attack, the ancient inner bolt soon succumbed. There was grunting below, a light flashed around the space. Darian shrank back and tried not to breathe. From far too close, a man's voice spoke. "We know you're in here."

Darian cowered, willing his heart to pause its roar.

"All right," the guard said, "grab the girl."

A muffled cry from Mariah.

"If you don't come out, we'll just take her."

They couldn't be serious.

"I'll go." Mariah's voice.

"She wouldn't be much use as a farm labourer. I'd say she'll end up at the barracks. Working nights, if you know what I mean."

The gathered men laughed. Darian forced himself to unstiffen. He crawled out from behind the chimney. "Get your hands off her," he growled.

The guard half in the hatch looked up and shone his light in Darian's eyes so that he had to blink. "Well looky here, see what slunk out of the dungheap." He beckoned once and slid out of sight.

Darian inched his way over to the hole and dangled his legs over the edge. Many hands seized his feet and pulled him down before he was ready to jump; he landed in a heap on the floor, but they hauled him upright before he could gather his wits.

Mariah stared at him, two guards still clamping her tight.

"Leave her," said the commander, and nodded towards the street, "Let's go."

They dragged Darian downstairs and out the door. The van waited in the street. As they opened it, Darian took a last look around—he surely wouldn't be back for a while. These homes and families would never be the same after this.

There was a movement at the corner—he flicked his eyes that way—Da! Too far to speak any words, yet none were needed. Someone grabbed him by the shoulder and shoved. "Get in."

He turned, and in doing so, spied Mariah on the front step, gripping Jemima around the neck. "She's yours now," called Darian. "Take good care of her." He climbed aboard, locked gazes with his father who approached at a run, then—slam. Only darkness from then on.

Darian continued to dig his section of field until his tears had dried. The memories returned every day, and every day he let them come, to strengthen his resolve to survive this place and get home again, one day soon.

He looked up and observed a commotion by the gate—must be lunchtime. Bucket in hand, he dropped his hoe and sprinted. He was the fastest runner on the field—had to be, since he liked the farthest corner.

He pulled up, only slightly out of breath, and was gratified to see plenty of food left in the pot. He dipped himself a bowl and slurped it with vigour.

Two of his nearby colleagues burst out laughing as they ate. He eyed them warily. "What's so funny?"

"You don't know what happened last night?"

"They brought a girl in to work here."

Darian gaped. "A girl?" He hadn't seen a girl for, well, six years. His sister had been the last.

"Where's yer eyes, man? She's on our team, marched in here this morning with the rest of us."

"In our field?" This must be some kind of joke. He scanned the team gathered to eat. "I don't see her."

"Maybe she missed the memo about lunch."

"It's her first day, after all." More laughs.

Another labourer leaned over towards the first two. "She's right pretty, so she is. I'd not mind stealing a wee kiss if I got the chance."

Juvenile giggles rippled around the group. Darian focused on getting his bowl perfectly clean, then, as slowly as he could get away with, he refilled his bucket with manure and made his way back to his far section. Slowly, this time.

There was no rush, after all. He just had to move enough so as not to catch a supervisor's unwanted attention, which occasionally led to punishments involving extra work, reduced food, or both.

Darian reached the place where he'd stopped before, set down his foul-smelling bucket, and raised his hoe at a precisely calculated speed that would cause no trouble.

His mind wandered, catching once more on those terrible memories of the day he left home. No—no, he didn't want to cry again. He'd shed enough tears for one day.

He cast about for other thoughts and came to land inevitably on his dog. He pulled a bittersweet smile. At least there was some sweetness in this memory. He pictured once more the day he'd first seen her.

The troubles had not yet come upon the land. The Senate loomed, but for the moment was only messing up America while the world watched, aghast, thinking that surely someone would step up and stop the madness. Darian, in his second to last year of high school, cared far more for making good grades and, alternately, for goofing off with the guys. Thus it was as he walked home from school that he debated with himself about the afternoon's plans. He could do homework—easy, if largely repetitive—or he could ask his neighbours Joe and Samuel if they wanted to go downtown and see what was happening. If they'd all enough pounds, they might buy a sandwich from Doorsteps & Co., for although the prices were exorbitant, the sandwich was a growing lad's dream.

Darian turned and ducked down an alley behind the mall—not an official shortcut, but an effective one. He passed the supermarket loading bays, several waste bins, a forklift sitting idle. Then a large cage filled with flattened boxes. He was almost out into the residential street on the other side when he heard it: a soft, distinct scrabble from the cardboard. Too small to be a person, too large for a bird or rodent.

Darian stopped in his tracks, approached the wire mesh container. "Hello?"

The scrabbling paused and there was a tiny cry that he couldn't quite identify. He tapped the wire so that it rattled. "Who's in there, hey?"

More movement, and a piece of cardboard shifted, revealing a small creature sheltering in the one box that had not been flattened.

"Mercy!" said Darian. "Who'd dump a pup in here?" For it could not have climbed the mesh walls by itself, even if there were a reason. The mostly black shadow mewled again.

"Well, let's see if we can't get you out." Darian shucked off his backpack, set it on the ground, and carefully folded his school blazer on top. He glanced around for something to climb on, and decided on one of the smaller wheelie bins, rolling it into position and rolling up his sleeves. "Okay, little one, I'm coming."

He gripped the sides of the bin and vaulted himself up to a precarious kneel. Raised himself slowly. Now he could grasp the edge of the cage and swing over, first one leg, then the other. He slid down to a soft landing on the cardboard, careful not to land on the pup. Reaching her hidey-hole, he extended a hand and drew her out. She trembled; instinctively he clutched her to him and felt her melt into his arms. His heart broke, and quiet anger burned against the perpetrators.

Holding the pup in one arm, he climbed back out and was just jumping down from the bin when the forklift driver appeared from behind his vehicle. "Here, kid! Whaddaya think ye're doin'?"

Darian turned to show his new burden. "This—this was in a box. In there." He nodded at the pile of cardboard.

The man's face softened. "Another one."

"This happens a lot?"

"Yeah, and I'd say we don't always find 'em before collection day. I just hope they didn't get turned into newspapers."

Darian felt sick. "What do I do with her?"

The driver rubbed his chin with thumb and forefinger. "Looks like she's yours now, chum."

Darian looked down at the wee bundle. She'd snuggled into his arm as far as physically possible, and tucked her nose into the crook of his elbow.

"Now go on home wi' ye. This ain't a public road, y'know." The driver flapped his hands and turned away.

Darian looked down once more, accepted his fate, and carefully bent to pick up his belongings with his free hand.

Slowly he walked home along the familiar streets of Castlereagh; the brick-fronted, terraced houses, the tiny front yards with their struggling greenery.

The tiny dog wriggled and he shifted his grip, but she was only trying to burrow even farther in than she had already. He clutched her tightly, muttering imprecations on the evildoer. "They don't deserve you." He reached his own street and turned in.

Sam loitered in the roadway. "What took ye so long? Ye comin' to town tonight?"

Darian shook his head. "Can't. Look what I found."

Sam approached. "Found?"

"Some idjit dumped her in a recycling bin."

Sam reached to fondle an ear, but the pup shrank back from his hand.

"Sorry," said Darian, "she seems to have attached herself to me."

"And your ma, what'll she say?"

Darian's face fell. Hadn't thought of that.

"You're about to find out, said Sam, and beat a retreat. Darian turned and met his mother, stoop-shouldered, returning from work.

"Hey, Ma," he said.

She looked up and smiled. "C'mere and let me see you."

He moved closer and turned so she could see what he held. She said nothing, only studied his face as he repeated his story.

"Well?" he asked, as they reached their own house. "Can we keep her? I mean, maybe just until I find someone to take her…"

His mother laughed. "My son, the dog rescuer."

The front door opened and fourteen-year-old Mariah bounded out. "Hullo! What's that you've got there?"

Darian passed over the pup with a brief explanation; the wee one seemed content enough with his sister. He looked back at Ma, who hadn't said anything one way or another.

"Food's expensive, you know. But I daresay you'll manage, if you buy less of them sandwiches." Her soft grin brightened. "D'ye think she can catch rats?"

Her children looked at her and back at the wriggling bundle in Mariah's arms, then all three burst out laughing. Such a beautiful sound...

...as it echoed in Darian's memories, adrift in a smelly field.

Thinking of Jemima's puppyhood carried him through to the end of the workday. He tossed his tools on the pile by the gate and filed out to march back to the barracks for dinner.

Encian Jack did not follow the team as usual. "You lot go on. I'll be there shortly."

Darian took the rare chance to walk slowly. Somehow today he was beyond caring whether there was any food left when he got to it. He stared up at the sky, at the almost-bare hills beyond the tall fences, and willed himself not to think of his mother—of how she'd died a couple of years after Jemima had joined the family.

He was pleasantly surprised to find some potatoes remained in the stew pot, and he took his portion. When he had eaten, he went straight to his bunk even though it would be light for hours yet. Sleep was the perfect escape from this place.

He was not ready for morning when it came. But then, he never was. Again it was the shuffle of colleagues that woke him. He dragged himself upright, did the necessaries, and joined the group by the breakfast tureen.

Darian was still eating when a murmur ran through the throng. He cleaned out the last of his porridge before he looked up.

Encian Jack had arrived to march them to the field—but who was that beside him?

Darian dropped his bowl, but no one noticed the clang, for all the others were similarly engrossed in the sight before them: a girl.

Suggestive chuckles broke out; yes, the same two who'd been

egging each other on at lunchtime. Darian returned his attention to the newcomer, who stared at the ground as if trying to sink into it. They'd been right about her being pretty, but all Darian wished was that she'd be spared from this awful place.

Encian hollered for attention. "Listen up! This 'ere's Andi Sumner and she's your new supervisor under my command."

Andi shrank even more into herself, hunching her shoulders. Encian kept talking. "You lot mind and do as she says, or we'll have to shift her to…other duties." He laid a hand on her back; she flinched away, eyes blazing.

"You fellas," she announced, "are going to be the most efficient team on this whole farm, or ye'll get what for from me."

Wow. For such a little person, she possessed a very big voice. Darian rubbed at his ears and watched her eyeballing each worker in turn. Finally her gaze landed on him and lingered. He refused to look away, and was surprised at the depth of desperation he read there. He could swear she was pleading, begging for help. He kept his regard steady and gave a slight nod. For a second he thought he saw the slightest hint of a smile, then it vanished and she was all business. "Right, men!" she screeched, causing more than a few winces. "Enough dallying, let's get a move on." She turned her head away as the team moved past her, but not before Darian glimpsed the moisture in her eyes—and right there, he determined he was going to make her life better.

the CLIMBER

Zhu Lee held the tin bowl carefully in both hands as she walked, sneaking a glance at its contents now and then as she paced the farm track some sixty kilometres from Paris. It was the usual cream of wheat they all ate, heavy on the bran as per regulations so that nothing would be wasted. But the head of the household, Aunt Wei, had added to this bowl a handful of precious raisins from last year's tiny grape crop. It was a miracle the vines still grew at all, and that it fruited was unheard of in this area. They kept the vines top secret for that reason, never allowing the Senate-assigned staff to care for them or go anywhere near the little grove of ancient trees that hid them. And so these raisins were the family's greatest treasure.

If she stayed with him while he ate, her father might even give her one. Zhu salivated at the thought and concentrated on her swift, sure-footed passage.

Slaves tended the fields she passed behind their low wooden fences—at this time of year, the work mostly consisted of watering the growing harvest and spreading fertilisers of various kinds. Here and there a Senate overseer watched the activity, but there were no shouts or threats.

Father had made it clear to the Senate people, when they'd arrived to help "increase efficiency", that things got done on this family farm, and yelling at folks wasn't going to improve things for anyone or increase the harvest. So their wheat grew as it always had, or nearly. It was not exempt from the worldwide dearth of viable seed. But Father managed the land, same as ever, using grain from previous years and carefully hoarded heirloom seed. That's how he still had grapevines—although the kitchen garden had long been relegated to history.

She was glad Auntie had served him raisins today. It was sure to make him smile, and Zhu had this morning decided to ask him something. Him being happy would certainly help.

Zhu reached the gate of the test field where Father experimented with batches of seed to find the best strains. He stood now at the far end, beyond the little plots marked off with string, hand on hip, rubbing his chin.

"Papa," she cried, unable to conceal her pride in him. Look at what he had done, even in these terrible times—even though in name the Senate had requisitioned the farm, Father's competence kept the family living on the same land, and together. Well, mostly. She bit her lip.

He turned, and his face lit up. "Light of my life! Is it so late already?"

She smiled at his banter as she drew near. "Look what Auntie sends you."

He took the bowl and frowned. "She is spoiling me. How many more raisins do we have?"

"Two cookie tins, I think."

"Well then, that is sufficient. Would you like to share?"

"Auntie will pour me a bowl when I get back, I'm sure." She took care to control her voice.

"Ah, but not with raisins, hey?" Father touched her chin, raised her face to look into it. "Sit with me."

They folded themselves to rest on the bare dirt of the path. Zhu kept her eyes averted from the food, though her stomach would soon be rumbling again. After all, she was here by Father's request and would leave when it pleased him to dismiss her. He spooned some of the thick wheaten gruel, a single raisin on top, and ate it, then held out the spoon to his daughter. With the utmost respect she grasped it and dipped a plain, ungarnished scoop.

"No, child, take one of these." Father reached for a raisin and with thumb and finger he deposited it on top of Zhu's spoonful. Slowly she brought it to her lips and emptied it. Closed her eyes for one blissful moment as the sweet fruit burst and made itself known to her palate. Finally passed back the implement and shook her head when Father offered more. For now, the taste of the raisin still lingered.

As he swallowed his last bite, she gathered her courage. "Father, I have a question."

"Anything, my sweet one." He set the bowl down and looked at her.

"I want to know what happened to Mother."

His expression darkened and she hurried to complete her speech. "Am I not old enough now?"

Her father sighed heavily and looked at his feet. "You are old enough."

Zhu's short fingernails dug into her palms. She would not press him.

Finally, he drew breath to speak. "You must ask your Auntie Wei. I was out in the fields that day, but she saw it happen. Besides…" His voice trailed off with a shudder, and resumed in a whisper: "…it is too painful for me to talk about."

Zhu had never heard the like. Her consternation grew as she discovered moisture in his eyes, and she threw herself at him. For a long moment they held each other, then he murmured again. "You are old enough. There are things you need to know, and we cannot protect you forever."

At this, she straightened, and gave her best curious look, but he would say no more. Quietly, she rose, took the bowl, and departed, her hand lingering on his shoulder. When she looked back from the field gate, he had not moved, his head barely visible above the swaying wheat.

Her stomach aflutter, she set her face towards the house. Perhaps she didn't want to know the tragedy that had formed and shaped her young life. Sooner than she imagined possible, she stepped into the kitchen, blinking in the relative dimness. She set the bowl and spoon in the sink and tried to vanish in the chatter.

"There you are, young one," said Auntie Wei, from her station at the stove. "Did your father enjoy his lunch?"

"He did, Auntie."

"What is it, child? You've gone pale."

"He said—Father said, that is—said you should tell me what happened to my mother."

Silence fell in the room. The other aunts and Zhu's two older sisters stared at her, their faces grim.

Auntie Wei's shoulders sagged. "Oui. It is time." She glanced at Lian and Yi. "I daresay your sisters were older when we told them, but these are perilous times."

Even her own sisters had not said anything to her? She shot them a dirty look, but was shocked to a gape at the way they clenched their teeth.

"Auntie," said Lian, "this is not right. She does not need to know. Not yet."

"Let her be innocent a while longer," pleaded Yi.

Lian snorted. "Innocent! Why, she is probably just saying this so that we tell her. Made up a tale to get a story out of us."

Zhu's eyes grew hot. "I did not make it up!"

"Then why did Father not tell you himself?"

"He—he could not. He was…weeping." Zhu's voice came out strangely strangled. The other aunts had stilled their work and watched the escalating exchange.

Auntie Wei swallowed. "You have the ring of truth, my dear. Do

128

not hold it against your sisters. They want only the best for you."

The dread turned sour in the pit of Zhu's stomach. "What is so terrible, then?" she shrilled into their shocked faces. "Did she die?"

"No," said Auntie Wei, "although that might have been better."

Most of the crowd shuffled out of the room, leaving only Auntie Wei and the three sisters.

"Quit beating around the bush and tell me what you know." Zhu was almost growling now.

Auntie Wei motioned to the table. When all were seated, she laid her hand over Zhu's, and began.

When she finished the sorry tale, Auntie added, "You take caution that the same doesn't happen to you."

That was the last straw. Zhu pulled her hand away and stared at the deathly serious faces. "You don't—you don't think I would—" She shot upright and ran from the room. In moments, she reached the bedroom she shared with her sisters—surely they would grant her its small privacy for now—and curled up on the floor. "My mama," she whimpered, and let the grief take her again, anew.

When she had exhausted her fresh supply of tears, she righted herself, wiped her face, and opened her drawer to retrieve a sheet from her precious stash of paper. Her stubby pencil must suffice. "I will write your story, Mama."

My mother was beautiful and gracious. Father was so proud of her in every way, so glad he had won her heart. She was so proud of me too, her last child heading off to school. I liked school and learned quickly, but often detoured slightly from the route home to climb the sandy cliffs of Mont D'Aigu. I felt so powerful when I stood on the top and surveyed the village from the heights. There is a road, of course, but it would have taken hours. This way I could climb up and scramble down and still be home before my sisters who went to high school already and would return later. I treasured those times alone with Mother, as she set out snacks and asked me how the day had been.

Then came the afternoon when I returned from my adventures and found the whole family crammed into the kitchen—aunties, sisters, Father. He sat slumped at the table, the womenfolk around him, but Mother was not there. They all stared at me; Father's face was haunted. "Little one, your mother has gone away."

That was all they told me. As the days stretched into weeks and then months, I knew she wasn't coming back.

The Senate had taken control of the government that year, but I did not care. I was seven, what did I want with politics? But now Auntie Wei has told me it meant absolute power for a few high-up officers in our area. It corrupted them, of course.

There had been a farm inspection, just routine, that morning. The officer had his aide write down the names of all who worked here. Father had pondered this as he returned to work in the field.

But scarcely an hour later, the officer had returned with a larger retinue in his truck. Mother and Auntie Wei had gone out to meet them, as was proper.

"Your services are needed elsewhere," said the officer. My mother was ordered to get in the truck, and when she hesitated, asked why, even as she wiped the flour from her hands onto her apron, they handcuffed her and lifted her bodily in. Auntie saw her frightened face once more as the door shut her away. The soldiers departed without another word of explanation.

Auntie says we cannot know what happened to her after that, but I see it in her eyes. I know my own experience, too—not long after her abduction, guards came to my school and transported the children to the new residential factories. I hid in a cupboard and escaped, ran home to Father, and have kept a low profile ever since.

Now I am fourteen and I can well imagine what soldiers might want with a beautiful woman. And that I am not safe, have not ever been, except for the small consolation that my name is nowhere on the farm's official records. Father left me off the list that day. Perhaps my mama is still alive out there, but like Auntie, I am not sure if I should hope that she is not.

Zhu folded the page and tucked it back into the bottom of the drawer. *I have to get out.* The grief would send her mad if she did not escape these walls and fences for a time. Her mind drifted back to the day Mother was taken, and the sandy cliff she'd climbed that afternoon and many since. *Perfect.*

She snuck out of the front door and away along the country road before anybody stopped her. With the shortcut she'd beaten through the woods, it was only a few minutes until she stood at the foot of the sandstone shelf. She flexed her fingers and looked up. Launched herself at the wall of rock, shot through with random roots and harder stones, all good for gripping and pulling.

She tested each handhold, many crumbling away at just a touch, and in this way progressed slowly towards the top. Near the end of the haul, she paused in a crevice to catch her breath. Gnarled tree roots surrounded it, reaching down from above, and the space between had eroded away. She surveyed the view, still partly blocked by the tallest of the old pines growing below. The top it must be, to see the whole valley.

Sufficiently rested, she swung back out onto the open sandstone surface. Not much farther now, but this last part was smoother, with less obvious handholds. She concentrated all her attention on the placement of her fingers, and when they encountered the flat top edge, she dug in her toes with one last effort and rolled over onto it, facing the view.

From up here, she could make out the homestead to the south, the village to the north, and farm after farm until the plains vanished in the eastern haze and the barely-hinted mountains that ringed the broad valley. She grinned and sucked in a slow, deep breath.

"Ahem."

The voice was right behind her. She seized the stubbly grass that grew on the outcropping and turned, not knowing what to expect, without even any time to formulate a thought.

A man towered over her, blocking out the sun. She blinked and recognised the hated uniform of a Senate guard, and two more looming behind him.

He crouched down so that the light blinded Zhu again and he drew a little to close for comfort. "Why are you not at work?"

She said nothing. What could she say that wouldn't incriminate herself or Father?

"Ah, perhaps you do not speak French, is that it?" His lips pulled wide, revealing large teeth.

"But I do," she finally blurted.

"You have no employment papers," he said, and it was a statement rather than a question. Again she did not answer. He glanced back to his colleagues, who took a step closer. "In that case we'll have to take you in, get you properly registered, and assign you a job." He reached out and stroked her hair, just once, but it sent a dirty crawling sensation down to her toes. He clenched his fist in the strands and pulled her closer, ignoring her yelp at the yank. "I'm counting on a finder's bonus. Don't worry, we treat our women well."

Like you treated my mother, she thought, and her mind became razor-sharp. She must escape. Right now she could not move, but he'd have to let go of her hair eventually…There! He loosened his grip to beckon his men.

Zhu grabbed her chance. She twisted her body back over the precipice, her feet waving in midair for a long moment while her fingers dug into the crumbling perimeter and her face swung perilously close to the guard's. Then her toe found purchase, and in a moment she was sliding below the rim, hands and feet easing onto the grips she'd known for years.

"Hey!" yelled the man, and reached for her, but she was already past his arms' length. She slid under an overhang, then another, and into the crevice where she had rested just minutes before.

Zhu paused and strained her ears. She took up a handful of pebbles and sand from the floor of the tree-cave and carefully dribbled them down the cliff-face.

There were shouts from above. "She's still headed down." Scuffles. Metallic pings—three, she thought—and the terrifying sound of a motor.

She listened as it bumped away down the mountain and swiftly became lost in the silence. Could she get all the way to the bottom and disappear in the woods before they arrived at the foot? Not likely. And she didn't want to head back up in case they had left one of their number there after all.

That left one option: stay right here and let them think she *had* escaped into the trees.

She dropped more stones in case there was anyone above to hear, then wriggled back into the cavity until her knees jammed into a root. She would be completely unseen from below, but could still raise her head and peer over.

Presently the van chugged into the open space in front of the cliff. All three men climbed out, to her relief. They stood around, pointing in various directions. One even indicated upwards. She shrank back, hid her face. Dare she wish for a miracle?

When she looked up again, it was to a distant whooshing of wings. Pigeons shot up from somewhere deep in the forest, over where the road ran through it.

The men below had seen it too. They gesticulated briefly, then leaped into the van and motored away.

Zhu laid her head down and cried silently. Safe! Maybe…but she would stay here until she was certain.

Eventually she dozed off, exhausted by terror and exertion. The crevice became shadowed and cool, and she relaxed into deeper sleep.

She woke with a start to moonlight on her face. She watched it rise, orange at first, fading to bright white that cast the landscape in starkly contrasted tones.

Time to assess her situation. She was well-slept, so that was a plus. On the minus side, she was stiff, sleepy, and hungry, and a drink wouldn't go amiss either.

She stretched her limbs one at a time in the tiny space. It would certainly be better to return to the clifftop, find another way off the mountain, and circle around to come at the farm from the opposite direction. Sigh. It was going to be a long, hungry walk.

She climbed the short distance slowly, cautious not to let even one scuffle mar the silence. When she grew level with the top, she paused to peer over and make sure it was safely abandoned. Once certain, she scooted across the space and vanished into the treeline.

It was hard to tell how many hours had passed, but the moon had passed its zenith and was sinking towards morning when finally she reached the southeast fringe of her father's fields. She paced along farm tracks between shining crops of young wheat, past Father's experimental field, and approached the sprawling house that held all her family and the workers.

But what was this? Lights and noise—the yard was full of people. Auntie, sisters, workers blinking in the headlamps. Headlamps? She squinted. Beyond them, the dreaded white van and the three guards, now holding rifles.

Zhu threw herself behind a rock. They'd gotten a good look at her face, of course they'd seek out "the Chinese farm" to find her. She would not be able to stay here—would have to hide out in the forest. Going away entirely was a thought not to be borne.

Her father's voice rang out, tired but determined. "As you have seen, Officer, all these people have employment papers. I think you should let these honest workers return to their rest."

Father! So brave. She feared for him, but apparently a manager's word carried some weight, for their followed only muttering, then the van doors shut and it roared away.

When it was quiet, Zhu dared peek around the rock. Auntie Wei was just ushering Yi into the house; the yard was empty but for Father standing erect in the moonlight. She sprinted, and he turned, sadness becoming delight on his face. She threw herself in his arms and buried her tears in his shoulder.

"Little One," he said, and held her tight.

ANGEL OF NORMANDY

The catch was exceeding good that day. Noah would eat well, and if he couldn't find anyone to trade with, he would just eat fish. It hadn't hurt him yet, though sometimes he wondered just how much salt was running through his veins. Oh well. It was much better than starving. He cast an eye over the dozen mid-sized grey mullets in the bottom of the boat and decided to try for one more, since they were biting so well. A big one this time.

He baited his line and threw it out, watching it slip into the deep green water. He was looking forward to getting home—back to his hidden shack on the coast, far from roads and prying eyes—where he would light a fire to cook and eat a feast of fish. Even if he was sick of the sight of it, he'd been out on the water all day and had built up a healthy appetite. He flexed one arm and smiled. No wasting away for him.

This last fish was taking a while to bite. Noah regarded the slack line, then the sea. He thought he could wait just a little longer. There were so many fish here today that one had to come along soon. He lost himself in practical thought—how much of this catch he would dry for later use, how many he would eat, how many he might have left to trade. He had only himself to consider—parents were a long absent memory and he'd been fending for himself for what felt like more than a lifetime or even two. When the Senate came, he'd seen them shipping people off to factories for slave labour, and decided to scarper before they could get a hold of him. Since then, he'd lived alone, far from civilisation, ghosting into the slave camps to trade fish for oats and sometimes potatoes, depending on what the workers were paid with. Not that it could really be called pay. His interactions with people had become covert, stolen just like the petrol for his boat. And so he had never had the chance to find a lover since, or start a family. Who would, indeed, in times like this?

A twitching of the line across his finger called him back from oft-repeated thoughts. A fish fought below; he fought back for a time, then pulled it in, flapping, on top of the others. Perhaps thirty centimetres. It was a good one. He smiled and looked up at the horizon: open water on one side, the bay opening on the other. The tide was well past turning, but he still had time to get home before the ebb emptied the bay completely.

Noah pulled in his sea anchor and readied his pride and joy: the little outboard motor that could propel his small vessel into the wide ocean and back to dry land. He pulled the cord and it roared into life. Hand on its tiller, he guided the boat between distant shores that narrowed in only slightly, ghostly as they were in today's haze. He passed by the abandoned Mont Saint Michel, its medieval towers poking the sky; the causeway still linked it to the mainland, but no one went there now. "Not even the angels," he muttered, with a glance at the hulking shape. It had gotten its name from an apparition of the Archangel Michael, who apparently had not liked it enough to return to his namesake island. Noah didn't blame him. Even an angel would have a hard time making use of a pointy, barren rock.

When it was behind him, he veered right and headed for shore— and in minutes, he could just make out the tiny creek mouth indenting the plain, where he had made his home.

But what was this? He squinted. Two large black objects swam up in the fog: military trucks? They'd found him!

Well, no. They didn't have him yet.

He cut the engine and for a moment there was only the slap of waves against the hull. Then—faint, but sounding clearly across the water: the barking of dogs. Had they followed the scent of stolen petrol?

His heart sped up and the sweat of fear broke out on his skin. Unconsciously, the fingers of his left hand moved to play across the bumpy scars on his right. Matching pairs of toothmarks that wrapped around his palm, from a long-ago encounter with a feral dog. He'd stayed well away from the beasts ever since, but the childhood trauma still visited his nightmares. In them, he felt even smaller than seven; in them, the dog grew to the size of a lion, and wolf-like although memory told him it had actually been a nondescript mixed-breed. It would go for his head, its maw full of shiny teeth, and he'd wake up soaked and breathing hard.

He shivered. Up until then he'd been planning to land farther around the coast and hide out until he could see the guards had left his home. But if they had dogs, the dogs would sniff out his return hike to the boat, and he would not risk that. People were not supposed to avoid being assigned to labour. They were also not supposed to pilfer petrol for unregistered vehicles, boat or no. He had good reason to expect severe punishment if caught.

Noah pulled out his oars with rowlocks attached and slotted them into their holes. Slowly, so as not to make any noise that might carry, he set his back and his bow towards the open sea. As he faced the shore in the traditional backwards rowing position, he could still make out the trucks as they stood by his camouflaged and invisible shack. Several small specks moved around: the guards themselves and possibly the dogs. He glanced to his right and noted the receding coastline passing by much quicker than his own two hands could row him—the bay's powerful tide had begun to ebb, pulling him outwards in its rush. There would be no return until it came in again, well into the hours of night. Noah considered his options. He could try to return home in moonlight; or stay out to sea an extra twelve hours so he could make the attempt in daytime. He screwed up his mouth and regarded his catch, already starting to pong. It would have to be eaten raw if he wanted to fill his stomach before gaining dry land. He'd done it before. He could do it again.

Resigned to a night on the Atlantic, he hoped it would be less choppy than the last time he'd ventured out into it. *Then again, this is the Atlantic we're talking about.* His heart sank. It was going to be a very long night.

But he wouldn't go back to face the guards and their dogs. If caught, and if the beasts didn't kill him outright, he'd undoubtedly be sent to a prison-like factory job and fed a starvation diet for as long as he managed to stay alive. No, he would far prefer to be his own man, out in the wild and on the water, even if there were days when the fish would not bite. He was proud that he could provide for himself—he could survive.

The tide pulled faster now, so that he barely needed to row. Soon he must pass under the Mount again. He turned to check its location and dug his right-hand oar into the brine just a little to adjust his course. Soon the rock loomed up over his left shoulder and he did not need to turn to see it. He peered at its towering blackness against the gently dusking sky, and at the dimming, deepening water skimming by him ever faster. A first larger wave crashed into his bow, sending spray across the interior. This night would not be fun.

Again his eyes strayed upwards to the haphazard shapes of the buildings coiled upon the island like a dragon. The abandoned island, where no one ever went—not even angels—those ancient walls that surely offered shelter more solid than he could ever build himself.

A patter of rain came on. He would soon be soaked through, and freezing to boot when the sea wind fingered his clothes.

That was it. He decided to make for the island, although he had no idea how to enter beyond its sea walls. There had to be an opening somewhere. He turned the boat and set to with the oars, but to no avail: the tide had a hold of him now and intended to sweep him out to sea.

With reluctance, he once more readied the engine, losing precious metres with the seconds it took. It responded sluggishly after an initial wet sputter. He paused to check how much juice was left; he'd have to steal some more soon, but for now, just getting to shelter would do.

Fighting the ebb, he approached the seaward side of the fortress. The walls were high here, impregnable above their rock foundation. He must go left or right…left would be safer in one respect, as it was the opposite side from his shack and less visible if the guards were still about; and yet it was the right side that he had passed many times and he thought he recalled seeing an indentation there not far from the causeway. What if there was only one place his boat could land? The causeway prevented a full circle by sea; he did not wish to retrace it in full dark.

He went right. Moved in closer to the rock, moved slower than he liked—the ocean resisted him mightily, but the little motor prevailed even if it was a close thing. He stared at the walls, scanning for any small anomaly, for the gap he thought was there.

He had made almost the entire half circle, and the causeway was well into view, when at last he spotted something like a dinghy-sized slot set into the wall. He aimed at it. This had better work. He dreaded the thought that he might have to let himself be carried out to sea after all.

Night came apace now and veiled his target, the moon not yet up. Noah blinked, squinted, listened for waves on stone. There…a rocky edge…a vertical corner…another. He eased the boat between and all was calm: no pull of tide, no splash of waves. Tall walls blocked out most of the remaining light from above.

When his eyes grew used to this extra layer of darkness, Noah perceived a rod set into the wall at the top and disappearing into the water below. This must mean he could moor safely through the changing tides. He soon attached the painter loosely to the rod, so it could slip up and down with the water level. Stone steps angled up around the cavity; he set a hand on one and found it slippery with algae. He packed the catch of fish into a bag that he then slung over his shoulder, and proceeded to crawl up the steps, one hand, one foot at a time.

With night coming on, he felt himself exhausted from his ordeal. He ducked into a doorway at the top of the steps and found a small room with a straw pallet, and, oddly, a water jug with a remnant in it. This he drank, brackish though it was; then he fell onto the mattress and into a deep sleep.

He did not know it when the ebb grew low enough for his boat to rest on sand at the bottom of its slot. He did not hear when it turned, rising again in due time; and he was still lost to the world when the waters once more began to go out, so many hours after his fishing trip should have ended.

He awoke to clear morning light, a man alone in a castle in the sea, a place he knew not at all even though he had seen it almost every day of his life. His throat was dry, his stomach growled. The first order of business must be to find water—surely they had wells or catchment tanks here somewhere—and a place to cook some fish. He shouldered his tote of now slightly dubious-smelling fish and stumbled out into the crisp brightness of the day.

Hungry and thirsty though he was, the movement of his body brought a different urge and he swiftly watered a crusty stem in a wooden planter box at the side of the street. For a street it was onto which he had emerged: a narrow, cobbled street that curved gently upwards around the conical hill. Two, sometimes three storeys of buildings encroached on the sky. Behind him, a sliver of mudflat showed through the archway, a piece of brownish plain and clean-washed sky above. He was glad the fog was gone, so he could see danger coming—provided he got above these buildings.

But first, a drink. Some rain had puddled on the ground and he wandered along until he found a cleanish windowsill carrying a weight of dew. He crouched to slurp it up. A few windows later, he was acceptably quenched and straightened to look more closely at the establishments he was passing. The rooms that opened off the street had once been shops or restaurants, and hotels lurked beyond and upstairs.

He pushed open a door to his right and entered a long room with a wide view over the bay. The floor-to-ceiling glass in the picture window was long gone, small spikes only remaining around the edges of the frames, but it comforted him to see so far. He passed by a selection of dining furniture, some pieces more broken than others, and as he approached the edge he seized a rickety chair frame. Another two steps, and he saw the void below for what it was—he had ascended higher than it seemed—no small drop from here. At a reasonable distance from the edge he broke up the wood by snapping it over his knee, and set it in a pile with some paper he'd found behind the bar. A flick of his lighter, and the fire came alive there on the tiled floor. He brought out his knife and cleaned a fish from his bag, flinging the guts and spine far out over the estuary. Gulls squawked as they fought over the remains far below. When the flame had burned white hot and quieted, he laid the strips of meat on the embers and watched closely. It sizzled, he turned it; minutes later, he pulled it out of the fire to cool a little. He ate quickly, watching the mainland the entire time.

Would they really not think to look for him here? Hiding in plain sight...perhaps it would be safe for a while at least.

He put out the fire and returned to the street, where he continued on his way along the incline. There were more businesses, plenty of hotels, a sandwicherie. Here he entered in search of supplies but found only an ancient jar of pickles in the back corner of a cupboard. Well, there might be many similar treasures in the neighbourhood. He set it in his bag and went on. A hotel lobby, entered out of curiosity, held nothing but a jewel-encrusted mirror that still hung on the wall. He regarded his own determined face in it, wondering what wealth had bought such extravagance in earlier times. Now, even pickles were worth more.

He thought he had rounded about a quarter of the island's circumference, and as much of its height, when the road came to an abrupt end. To his left, a vast, arched staircase straight up to the heart of the mount; to the right, a crenellated turret. He walked out to the turret's indented rim and stared at the northern coast of the bay, still and silent in the distance. Nothing moved but the seabirds and the tide far away to his left.

When he had looked his fill, he turned his face to the stairs. Onward and upward, then. He climbed—ten steps, thirty, a hundred…he lost count. Finally, breathing a little harder than usual, he emerged onto a wide paved expanse bordered by a wall. He approached it, and thought, oh yes, this is high up all right. The plains came up through the morning light, shimmering in the distance, the farmlands barely tinged in green, vanishing in a delicate haze at the horizon. He could see the river Couesnon, the mainland settlement, even the small bay where his shack stood.

The elevated plaza looked west and south and east; on its north loomed a church, the only thing higher than where he stood now. Several doors were set into its wall besides the main one, and he peered inside them all: storage closets, mostly, full of brooms and spiders, but at one he stopped and gaped.

For here was more opulence than he had seen in all his life together, The walls were hung with tapestries, several velvet couches alternated with carved mahogany chests. He lifted a heavy lid, caressed the warm clothing within. A fireplace occupied the back wall of the apartment, and a small window facing east. He blinked at the thick red pile of the rug, kicked off his shoes, and let his toes sink in as he crossed to the window. The settlement and indeed most of the causeway was visible. He picked out the place his shack was hiding. Had the guards and dogs left it alone now? Perhaps it didn't matter any more. From here he would see trouble coming—at least in daylight.

Satisfied, he allowed himself a grim smile and turned to survey the room once more. His new home? Yes, he thought he could live here. He would survive between fishing and fossicking, and soon this place would give up the rest of its secrets to him.

He spun slowly in a circle, raising his arms, and spoke to the room. "Now I shall be the angel of this place!"

ChilDREN OF WALES

The dawn came apace and reached its fingers through the sacks that hung over the windows of the hut. Rowena Tally watched as the minute hand moved into the vertical position, sighed once into the morning silence, and tapped her younger sister on the forehead. "Six o'clock, little one."

She wound the old watch with care, as she did every morning. They couldn't lose track of time—lateness was not tolerated by their employers. It wasn't just an empty threat; she'd seen people dismissed for less than minor infractions. She breathed the still air and regarded the sleeping form for just a moment longer. It was no use envying her sister's stronger build and constitution; it would only bring a harder work assignment.

"Come on," said Rowena, and poked Anna again. The only response was a groan. Anna, sixteen, threw her arms across her face and growled. She loved her sleep, although that fondness could not be limited to teens. Rowena tried to smile about that, but it came out as a grim tightening of the lips.

Rowena dug her fingers into Anna's shoulder and shook. Anna

roused herself to her elbows and a wordless glance passed between the two of them—a glance, Rowena thought, that carried much in the way of shared suffering. No matter the ten-year age gap. They were all each other had left.

Quickly they dressed and gulped some water, downing a bite or two of last season's pumpkin that had managed to grow despite all odds against it. It had been roasted over the fire a few days ago but was still fairly acceptable to eat.

"Might need to finish that up by tomorrow," remarked Anna. She swirled the dregs with a handful of water and swallowed.

Rowena just nodded and swallowed the last of her breakfast. That would have to keep her going until her government-mandated portion at noon.

At six-fifteen they stepped out into the day. Rowena liked summer, when they did not have to walk to and from work in the dark and cold. The sky was still pale, washed clean by overnight showers, and a westerly wind carried the sound of the sea from the direction of the cliffs. It would be beautiful at the beach today, especially as the day progressed and the sun would creep over the cliffs to shine fully on the expanse of sand.

She didn't notice she'd stopped to sniff the air until Anna tugged on her arm. She opened her eyes and turned with great reluctance away from the coast, just a solid half-hour's walk from here. But work was farther than that, for both of them, almost exactly in the opposite direction.

They paced along the rutted track—thankfully not too muddy this time of year—until it became a gravel strip. Neighbours fell in with them, each acknowledged with a nod or a word and heading in the general direction of distant Haverfordwest. Times might be rough, but the Cymry, the people of Wales, still greeted life with a smile. For now at least.

Anna topped a hill just ahead of Rowena, and the intersection came into view across the next valley. From there, Anna would continue straight ahead past the caravan park to join her construction crew at the new factory near the village of Walwyn's Castle, being built to provide a living for the many local people who had none. And Rowena would turn left along the road to the fish processing plant at Little Haven.

"Are you going to pay your visit on the way?" Anna asked.

Rowena nodded. It was a question often asked, and the answer had always been the same. She wasn't sure if Anna thought there'd be a change of mind some day. For herself she was sure that couldn't be the case.

Soon they crossed the stream at the bottom of the dip and began to climb the ascent towards the turnoff.

Just as they reached it, the sisters exchanged a hug like they usually did, but Rowena was surprised to find Anna still grasping her shoulders.

"Have you ever thought..." Anna's voice wavered, then became more confident. "It might be time to leave it behind?"

Rowena's heart twisted. "Oh, Anna, not you too? That's what they all say to me at work."

"And you don't think they have a point?"

"They haven't had it happen to them."

"We've all lost someone."

"Not the same. Not the same." Rowena pulled away and forced herself to breathe calmly.

Anna reached for her again. "It's been eight years. Won't you leave it behind? We need all our focus for here and now."

"She's not an it." Rowena held Anna's concerned gaze with a determined one of her own.

After a long moment, Anna looked down. She patted Rowena's arm and nodded. "I just don't like how consumed you are, after all this time."

Rowena gulped, managed a hint of a smile although there was no heart in it, then backed away, turned and ran without looking back. She slowed when she was sure Anna had gone on out of sight and continued at walking pace while she regained her breath. The land was mostly flat here, with only gentle dips and rises; the road was hemmed tightly by low hedges that harboured only a little life now, dry and brittle as all plants had become.

It wasn't that she didn't want to let go. Rather, that option simply was not a choice she could make. Rowena passed two grey stone houses and turned right, passing a cluster of derelict barns and more scattered homes.

She had regained most of her equilibrium by the time she reached the little copse that marked the place. She stepped off the road, padded through soft earth, and emerged into a clearing studded with mounds and markers.

The sun shone through the trees, casting long morning shadows and bright rays. Rowena thought something moved far out in the field, but it must be a trick of the light and the dancing boughs. Watching her feet, she picked her way along the familiar path.

When she was nearly there, she looked up and almost leaped backwards. A boy sat at her destination, hugging his knees, staring at the marker.

Rowena's eyes strayed there too by habit, and just like every day, she read the words she'd carved into the wooden crosspiece: *Lynda. My daughter. 20.02.2071.*

Blinking, she looked back at the boy and realised he was not holding vigil at Lynda's grave, but the next one over. It held a woman's name and two dates, one of them just this year. She thought she vaguely remembered when the new grave went in, when the earth had been disturbed and a fresh, unweathered marker placed at its head. But although her visits were regular, they had to be quick, and she had not considered the name beyond a first, cursory glance. Not that she knew the lady. Now, though, she thought about the dates and regarded the boy again.

"Your mother?" she asked gently as she knelt on the scrubby grass.

The child nodded, and turned his head to Lynda's grave. "Your baby?"

The understanding in his voice wilted Rowena's composure and she flung up a hand to cover her face. Soon, slim fingers gripped her wrist and pulled it clear. The small, earnest face hovered close to hers. "We don't ever stop missing them, do we?" he said.

"No. No, we don't." She opened her arms because his presence demanded it, and he fell into her embrace. A small sob shook him and it was all she could do to keep her own tears inside. "Oh, child. Who are you? And who's taking care of you now?"

He wriggled around and leaned back on her, looking up into her face. "No one, really. I mean—just me. Tristan. It's pretty rough. I'm always hungry."

Rowena was about to give the standard answer—everyone's always hungry—but took another look at the spindly arms and legs, the sallow skin, the tired eyes that were, however, still bright.

"You're all on your own?"

"My uncle lets me sleep in his shed, but he doesn't share his food. Fact is, he doesn't have any."

Rowena's mind raced even as she struggled to accept the child's simple affection.

"Listen," she said, "if you wait for me here about six-thirty I'll bring some food." She'd have to save some of her lunch from the fish factory.

The boy's face lit up and he hugged her tight.

"Before you get all excited, it's not that great. At my work they basically feed us fish guts."

He blinked, but showed no disgust. Good kid.

"All right then. I'll see you here a bit later on." She reluctantly nudged him off her lap and stood; he rose unsteadily and wrapped his arms around her waist. One by one she pried his fingers away, sighing.

"Can I not walk with you a wee way?" His eyes, how big they were! Like pools. And how they fixed her in place.

She nodded. "If ye've the strength."

He burst into a cascade of delighted giggles, and he grasped her hand as they left the graveyard. "I've told you my name. What's yours?"

"I'm Rowena."

"Rowena." He rolled the syllables around in his mouth, grinned again, and set his face to the path where the stick-like trees cast swaying shadows.

Out in the narrow road again, Rowena had to extend her pace so she would reach her place of work in time. The boy kept up bravely for several minutes, then stopped abruptly, pulling her up short. She turned to face him. "I'm sorry, Tristan-bach, I can't go any slower or I'll be late and lose my job, or worse."

"I—I understand." He squeezed her hand and let go. "I'll see you after, then—well, back there."

"That you will." Time was marching, so she resisted the urge to hug him one more time, instead waving as she turned away.

The hedgerows blurred before her. But it wouldn't slow her down. The road narrowed even more, hemmed in tightly on both sides, leading ever onwards to the day of drudgery for a bite to eat. *What have we come to…*

Finally, the hedges gave way to a more open landscape bordered by low stone walls, and her first glimpse of the sea for today. Caravans loomed up to one side, a residential community. It would be nice to live there, just far enough away from work to forget it for a while. But these spots were reserved for larger families, the ones with children.

Lynda. My heart. She blinked hard. *Lynda's not here.*

The road met the clifftop and the blue-green sea spread out below her. She smiled and inhaled deeply. This was her favourite part of her daily walk. A short section, to be sure, but no less enjoyable for it. There was a path down there, nearer the edge, that she sometimes took when she had more time, or on the way home. She would not be seeing it today, she thought with a wry grin. Roofs nestled into the slopes opposite the sea, and buildings thickened as she went. Nearly there. She passed the stretch where the road had been dug between high banks holding tall, straight trees that had somehow managed to cling to life.

Soon the houses of Little Haven appeared over their black hedges, more and more until there were no gaps at all—the diminutive homes lined up wall to wall. Despite the ravages of recent years, the village had retained some of its old-world Welsh charm. Round a few more corners, and there it was: the short beach and beside it, the Castle: once a pub of some renown, now repurposed as her place of servitude.

Rowena nodded to a few of her colleagues who waited on the seawall. She joined them and looked out to sea for the return of the fishing boats, the signal for their work to begin. The crowd swelled to almost a hundred. Rowena looked around, hoping nobody was missing—the consequences were not worth it, no matter the reason.

"There they are!" someone called, pointing at the horizon. Sure enough, one shadow followed another, four boats in all. The crowd of workers surged into action. Some leapt the several feet to the stony shore, while most hurried across the tiny bridge and down the ramp to the sand. All came to the water's edge and watched as the boats chugged in, bearing weary souls and the morning's catch. One by one each skipper beached his flat-bottomed chugger, and those aboard set about passing down the huge plastic crates of fish.

Rowena waited her turn and was duly weighted down with a smelly burden. A small black wrasse still flapped about, and she regarded it only for a moment. There was no discrimination in death: here were pollack, bass, trout, cod and mullet. Eels were regular too, and once she'd even seen a thornback ray. She lugged the crate back up the ramp, over the bridge and under the Castle's lintel. She heaved it onto a table where the row quickly grew. But they couldn't start processing yet, not until all the fish were brought in. Twice more she went outside, and when she returned the third time, the room was already abuzz with work.

She approached one of the supervisors and was given a gutting knife, with which she went to a table and reached for her first victim of the day, slapping it down on the wooden surface where food and drink had once been served to commoners who had not been starving. She knew this, because she had been one of them, before the world changed.

Setting her knife at an angle behind the mullet's head, she sliced off a clean fillet, flipped the carcass over, and did the same on the other side. The boneless pieces she threw in the white bucket, the head and bones in the black one. Both would be emptied in due course: the white to be frozen and sent to the cities, and the black to be cooked down for the locals.

The hours passed slowly, her breakfast long since absorbed, her stomach making its usual complaints. But she was pleased with herself, no accidental knife wounds today. So far. Somewhere in the back, their fish soup was cooking, and as tired as she was of the flavour, her mouth still watered.

Finally, someone called out that it was ready, and table by table the workers lined up to receive a bowlful. It was probably mostly water, but it was hot and filling. She tucked her knife into her pocket and approached the kitchen in her turn.

Now, the real question: how was she going to keep some of this and take it with her for Tristan? Desperate times called for desperate measures. She drank all the liquid out of her serving and eyed the whole fish head in the bottom. It eyed her back with a dead stare. Before she could reconsider, she grabbed it and shoved it in her pocket, then returned the bowl to the kitchen.

The new cook, an intensely practical, no-nonsense blonde, took it from her and cast a glance at the spreading wet patch on her old jeans. "Oh, dear," she said. "That won't do at all, at all."

No! She'd been discovered. She found herself rooted to the spot, unable to move, terrified the punishment would be worse if she tried to run away.

In a moment the cook returned, a greased canvas sack in one hand and a water jug in the other. "Give me what you've got in there," she commanded.

Rowena could only obey, handing over the slimy head. *I'm sorry, Tristan.*

The cook barely glanced at it. In one movement she shoved it inside the sack, then without warning she threw the water at Rowena's lower half, laughing as Rowena gasped. "There, dolls, now nobody will know what you tried."

"There's—there's a child…"

"There always is." The cook shoved the sack into Rowena's hand. "Best be hiding this."

Rowena gaped. It was too heavy to contain just one fish head. She yanked at the neck of her shirt and shoved it into her bra. Good thing she'd worn a high-fronted tank top. "Thank you—"

"Hush now. Time to get back to work."

The two exchanged a hint of a smile, then turned carefully around. Nobody paid any attention. Rowena moved back to her work table and took up her knife again, joyfully launching herself into her task. She was suddenly grateful that her underwear was both shapeless enough and stretchy enough to accommodate these few handfuls of nourishment without too much of a bulge.

The afternoon passed in the usual haze of weariness, and Rowena corrected her posture many times, only to discover again and again that she had returned to a slump. Soon her toil would be over and she could straighten herself out on her walk home. And Tristan…what was she going to do about that boy? There was food enough for today, perhaps one day at a time was good enough for now.

Finally she reached into her last fish crate and found it empty. She raised her arms over her head and stretched a few kinks out of her frame.

"You can go," said the supervisor behind her.

Rowena almost jumped out of her skin. "Um, thanks."

But the boss didn't move on. He leaned in a little too close and smirked at her. "Kid, you smell like fish."

I'm not a kid. But all she said was, "We all smell like fish in here." She hoped he couldn't hear the quaver in her voice or suspect the contraband on her person.

"That's right, keep your sense of humour." He patted her shoulder and indicated the door. "What are you waiting for?"

This time her smile was genuine. She made her escape, darting through the little town like her pants were on fire. Once on the inland road, she was able to relax more. But what an adventure. She hoped that cook wouldn't get in trouble.

The distance flew by under her eager feet, and soon she pushed in at the entrance to the little graveyard. Around another couple of bends in the road, Anna would be waiting—*just a little longer, dear Anna.*

Tristan sat by the crosses, his golden head resting on his knees.

"I'm back," called Rowena, and he shot to his feet and ran to her, a surprising amount of energy.

His arms wrapped around her and she lost her balance. Laughing, they collapsed in the grass and she drew the sack out of her shirt.

Tristan's eyes grew round. "For me?"

"For you."

Rowena watched as he reached in and pulled out a boiled fish head. Warily he bit into it, slowly at first, then with all the efficiency of a vulture.

"Be careful of the bones. You don't want to eat those." Rowena pointed one out for him.

He finished the first fish head, sucked the bones, and licked his fingers, then leaned against Rowena. "You know," he said into her shoulder, "Lynda would have been eight now. I'm nine. I think I would have been her friend."

Rowena clutched the back of his head. She bit her lip.

Tristan went on. "You lost your baby. I lost my mam. Do you think we could…"

She couldn't speak past the lump in her throat for all the lost children of Wales, herself included. His hand found hers in the silence of the day's golden glow.

"I think you're right," she said, at last. "You would have been great friends with my Lynda."

the Beast of Ulster

Fiona Butler, cyborg guard, clunked along her patrol route. Her legs whirred as her integrated visual circuits cued up a list of maintenance threads for her CPU to run through. Only Fiona could see the green bar moving through its progression. Tonight's route took her through the tightly-packed residential streets of inner-city Belfast near the railway station, mostly made up of squat terraced buildings which had in earlier days been homes to one family each. Now it was more like one per room. She rounded a corner, heard a scuffle ahead—but it was only a dog dodging from one alley to another. Though she certainly could if she wanted to, there was no need to shoot the dog: curfew applied only to humans. Checking her weapons nonetheless, she continued on her way.

She patrolled alone tonight, word having come through from the higher-ups that she and McDermott ought to divide their attention to cover more streets. Much as she hated to admit it, she missed their easy banter and being able to share this ultimate power with another human being.

If the two of them could still be called human, that is. With a thought, she checked for the thirty-fourth time this hour that the bullets were ready within her metal hand. She felt something in her eye and almost reached to rub it away, stopping herself just in time. There *was* something in it—delicate wiring that she should not touch even when it became uncomfortable. She could unplug the shades during her recharge, although even then the connector would remain firmly attached to her ocular nerves. It was painful and inconvenient, but still infinitely preferable to the life she'd led before: always hungry, and prey for the predators in her extended family. *Now, I am the predator.*

She'd only balked a little to hear that becoming an invincible cyborg would mean losing an eye and three of her limbs. Getting away, it turned out, was more important. The replacements were strong, though heavy, and she'd had to work her torso muscles hard to gain the ability to carry herself and become an efficient agent of the Senate. It was all worth it. *Look at me now*, she wanted to shout across the years at those who had harmed her. In fact, she'd rather like to meet them one quiet night. On patrol, she had full jurisdiction. Her superiors would not question a swift execution she deemed necessary.

This is a good life, she told herself yet again. *Here, I reign supreme.* She didn't like the wheedling voice of her self-talk, her victimised nature like the little girl she used to be—she was practically the toughest person in Belfast now, and had nothing to fear from anyone. So why did the words in her head sound like she was trying to convince herself of their truth? The common people would no doubt cringe to think of what had been done to her body in the name of progress. But she was one of just a few chosen. She was her own person now more than ever before, no matter what anyone thought, and if every day of her life was marked by her murders, then so be it. *But it's not murder if they broke the law.* At least that was what her employers said. She wasn't about to jeopardise her position by disagreeing. Besides, sometimes it felt good to kill.

Fiona moved along Friendly Street without incident, letting her eyes trail along the solid row of brick houses, all the same colour but for graffiti here and there, and the varying rates at which they crumbled. Her vision picked out hundreds of human-sized heat sources behind the walls, so many that they swam and merged before her. How many people lived here? She called up the registry data from her internal server and blinked. Thirteen hundred and eighty-three! Why, that was more than ten per unit. Three to a room, at least. She was suddenly glad of her solo bunkroom back at the station. At the dead end she slipped through a gap between the buildings and continued to wend her way around the neighbourhood. There was not much to distinguish any of the streets; only the map on the heads-up display inside her shades told her where she was.

Her circuit of this residential enclave completed, she crossed the highway and moved on into the centre of town, where the buildings were taller, winds eerier, the silence of curfew tempered by the fact that thousands of residents were at this very moment inside the apartment blocks that surrounded her. She let her feet fall heavily, ensuring the plebs would hush at her approach. The more aware people were of her, the more reluctant they'd be to sneak out after dark and risk her dispassionate judgment.

She passed an ornate church, now used for something else, she couldn't recall what. A glance at the database told her it was a food storehouse. The exterior was dark, but there would be armed guards inside, keeping safe the rations that the people would be given at their workplaces—provided those workplaces were not themselves food processing plants with their own supplies of whatever they produced.

Something flickered in her peripheral vision. She glanced up at the dim windows of the next building. A curtain was quickly drawn across to block her sight, but her heat-tracers spied the outline of a child cowering beyond. She smirked. *Diddums wanted to see a cyborg, hmm?* Perhaps the stolen glance would put the proper fear into him.

Leaving the taller blocks behind, she passed ordinary houses again. They were all the same…like sausages out of a machine, though that sort of food had not been made for many years now. She inspected the house fronts, finding them only slightly changed from the ones she'd patrolled earlier. These were smaller, with only two windows on each façade and made of the same red brick that was the essence of Belfast. An occasional building had its upper floor painted white instead; some had different framing.

She sighed. *Boring, boring, boring.* But she wouldn't think like that. Couldn't. It was infinitely preferable to before.

Fiona reached the district of Shaftesbury and entered the warren of little streets. When she got to a small triangular park near its middle, she paused and listened to the clatter of the bare branches on the trees. No one had cut them down for firewood yet, oddly enough. Maybe someone was still hoping they would come back to life. She didn't think it likely.

There was a rustling from within the ailing stand of birch. She inched closer. Surely that was too big to be a dog or cat. Fiona shifted one metal foot forward, and it clunked loudly. She winced. Just when she thought she'd gotten her new appendages under control.

Scrambles reached her ears, then silence. Someone would be attempting to avoid discovery about now. Fiona flicked up an internal display and used an eye movement to switch to precision control. She circled the copse, coming to view it from the opposite direction. Now completely silent, she was able to creep right up and peek through the trees.

It was a young couple, their arms still entwined, peering out to where they'd heard her step. "False alarm," said the bloke.

"Yeah but what was that then? We heard something, so we did."

"Sure. But whatever it was…is gone." He returned his attention to his lady love. "Let's not get too distracted now."

"Ach, ye talk like I'm something special."

"But you are."

The girl made embarrassed sputters as he dared to touch her cheek. At this, she melted into him. "Oh, George," she said. "I amn't sure this be a good idea. With the world the way it is, and all."

"Let's be happy for as long as we can."

Fiona continued to watch without giving herself away. She was both drawn and disgusted by the spectacle. As a little child she'd dreamed of getting married someday, but the experiences in between had stolen her desire for that outcome. It was not what she wanted now, although she assumed she could probably have any of the guards she chose—they would not dare refuse one such as her. An idea to play with later.

For now, she had other amusements. The two before her were unaware that she was observing, which meant she would be able to choose how to reveal herself for the biggest laugh. Later, of course. The public shouldn't see a cyborg laughing, as curfew was not a laughing matter. That is, if she let them live past the next couple of minutes, which was not a certainty in the slightest.

She took a clinical view as they whispered sweet nothings. Their lips brushed, once, twice, then met and maintained contact as their bodies moved in the age-old dance that would inevitably lead to more. Fiona noted the caresses, the stroking of the hair, the gripping of the shoulders and arms. Wouldn't they need to breathe soon?

Eventually they withdrew to what was in fact still quite a close proximity, and with her infrared enhancements Fiona observed their elevated temperature readings. They must be quite high on pheromones.

Suddenly, the male became focused. His knees hit the mucky dirt as he manoeuvred to reach his trouser pocket. Fiona watched, fascinated, as he withdrew a small, obviously homemade cardboard box that fit in the palm of his hand. It was constructed of a weathered piece of something that had once been printed, though most of its glossy coating was gone. Tiny, irregular laminate shapes still glinted there in the minimal light. It had been cleverly folded to hold itself in a box shape. Fiona eyed it. For a moment, she thought she remembered a story she'd heard as a child, of kneeling and boxes and a man and woman. But she couldn't remember it properly, and being as it had happened well before her augmentations, the data was not stored where she could access it. So she continued to watch. What might this box hold, and why was he bringing it out when he surely had more interest in continuing with physical affection?

The female appeared to guess something, for her hands flew to her cheeks. Fiona's infrared spectrum detected additional heat even beyond what had arisen during the kiss.

The male cleared his throat. "Hrm. This is for you…because I want to marry you. Will you have me?" He slid the top part of the box upwards to reveal, nestled inside, a knotwork ring with a small greenish stone. The type that cheap tourists had bought by the thousands in the days of old. It certainly wasn't gold, or anything precious, but it had a huge value as a symbol of what used to be. Why, a family could probably be fed from it for a week or two, Fiona mused.

The girl extended her hands and wrapped her fingers around his as he held the box. This was the moment Fiona chose to intervene.

"I'll take that," she said, and stepped through the last layer of branches.

The reaction couldn't have been more textbook. Their hands frozen in place around the box, the two jerked their heads towards her and gaped, trembling like terrified mice. "I—I'm sorry about the late hour, miss," said the male, his voice tremulous. "I just needed some privacy for this here personal matter."

"You've got nerve," Fiona admitted. And *Miss?* She hadn't been called that since she was little. *Snort.* She took another step, now within reach of the couple. They shrank back. Understandable, since she was mandated to shoot them. She reached out with her metal hand, eliciting a sort of gasping sob from the female, and took the ring out of its sad little box. Dropping it into the palm of her real hand, she ran her eyes over the ancient pattern that formed it: one single thread, weaving back through itself to form a triple-wide cord. She ran her thumb over its relief, where the gold colour had mostly rubbed off to reveal the alloy beneath. Cheaply made, for sure, but it was still a real token of the designs that had been used for hundreds of years since the times of far ancient Ireland. "How did you pay for this?"

He dropped his eyes and heat rose in his face. "I, um, ran a lot of errands for a rich guy."

"One of those crime lords in the docklands, eh?" Fiona laughed at the girl's horrified face. "So you've been aiding and abetting the black market."

She closed her fist over the ring and raised her other index finger—the metal one that would shoot the bullets to end these lives for breaking curfew.

The female whimpered again and buried her face in the male's shoulder. He gripped her around the shoulders, their hands still clasped around the box, fingers tightened so much that it collapsed.

Fiona looked at the ring again. There was no hurry, after all. It called to something deep inside her, as if its origins were meshed with hers—perhaps an ancestor had created the original pattern centuries ago. It spoke to her of other times and people who had not lived a tormented life.

She glanced up at the couple, clinging to each other even with their lives about to end. They could not be allowed to survive this—she had her reputation to think of. They didn't call her the Beast of Ulster for nothing.

What was she even thinking? She checked the bullet in her finger. She would need another immediately after it, and she blinked at her menu again. Readied the quick-load protocol, its soft clicks resounding down her arm.

The young man raised his head slightly, still comforting his lover where she cowered in his arms. He levelled a steady gaze at Fiona.

Gah. She hated when they did that—so she rarely gave them a chance. It wouldn't happen again.

The ring became heavy in her palm and she realised she had made a decision. She lowered her gun hand. "If you breathe a word of this," she growled, "I will find everyone you know and I will kill them. Slowly. While you watch," she added, shooting a finely-honed blade out of her middle finger. "After that, I'll think up an *extremely* interesting conclusion to your pitiful lives."

The female flinched, but remained quiet. The male continued to stare at her. Without understanding why, she tossed the ring at him. He caught it without looking away from her face. For a moment, she mustered her best glare, but realised he would not be able to see it behind her shades.

"Gerroutofit," she growled, and the spell broke. The two scrambled to their feet and launched themselves out between the trees. When their running footsteps had faded to silence, Fiona rubbed her creased brow with her flesh hand. She was getting soft. *Well, one monkey don't make a circus.* She was still the Beast of Ulster.

Exiting the park area, she continued on her beat, her thoughts awhirl. She must not doubt herself; she must not cower before her required tasks of murder and intimidation. Then she knew: she must wipe this incident from her memory. *Damn.* The thing she hated most was to discover something had been deleted, but it was the only way to ensure she remained a perfect killing machine. Still, she would not do it immediately.

She called up a map and navigated to the nearby docklands, where she settled to sit on the edge of a wharf. A ferry lay half-sunken a stone's throw away, one of the fast ones that used to go to Scotland in just one hour. Now Scotland might as well be the other side of the world. Fiona regarded the dark water between her metal feet as they hung over the side. If she ever wanted to end this measly existence, she was sure water would do it: her metal parts were too heavy to float, and immersion would cause her augmentations to short-circuit so that she would be effectively paralysed and sink, with drowning soon to follow, and she'd become just another shipwreck. That is, if the hard-wired anti-suicidal circuits would even allow her to try. She shivered. She still needed air to breathe, and that was not a way she wished to go. *I definitely need this memory wiped.*

For a moment longer, she allowed herself to feel the longing that had rushed into her when she held the ring with its ancient swirls. It felt good just to wish for better times, even if she would never experience them.

The clouds parted, allowing starlight to beam through and twinkle on the surface of the waters. All was silent, as it should be.

Fiona sighed and began to assemble the coding she would need for the memory operation. It must self-delete when it had run its course, so that there would be no incriminating evidence in her automatic report. With any luck, it would only show as a common glitch in recording. *Activate.*

She found herself looking at her map in the heads-up display. Why was she off her route? She'd have to walk a little faster to complete her assigned streets for tonight. There better not be anyone around—she felt distinctly merciless.

The image of an elaborate Celtic knotwork design flashed into her thoughts and she frowned. Where had that come from? Probably just the circuitry, doing a number on her imagination.

Fiona shook her head and walked on. Superimposed on city streets, her mind traced the paths of the endless knot that always came back to its beginning, on and on, infinite.

Her feet echoed on the concrete of the road as she strode out powerfully, watching candlelight in curtained windows extinguish at the sound of her passing.

Here, I reign supreme.

about the author

Grace Bridges is a dreamer whose muse blows best when it's fresh from the sea. A graduate of the University of Auckland, she edits novels and translates German for a living, and writes from her hilltop in New Zealand although faraway places call to her just as often. Her writings appear in various international anthologies and magazines, and she is working on further novels and short stories in The Vortex of Éire series and others.

www.gracebridges.kiwi

How far would you chase hope?

What if you could change the world?

The green has gone from Mariah's Ireland.
Every garden and field that was once lush with crops is now
lifeless muck. And yet Mariah holds one seed...the seed of
hope to feed the hungry.

Together with Liam, her staunchest supporter, Naomi the
biologist, Deborah, whose son sold out to the Senate, and
Peter the farm boy, she sets out to make Ireland green
again. That is Mariah's hope. It is Mariah's dream.

Mariah's dream will change everything.

www.ingramcontent.com/pod-product-compliance
Lightning Source LLC
Chambersburg PA
CBHW021046130626
46552CB00005B/2033